Books in the Cary Redmond Series

The Trouble with Black Cats and Demons
The Trouble with Ghouls and Serial Killers
The Trouble with Leopard Queens and Shifter Wars
The Trouble with Baby Gods and Vampires
The Trouble with Magic and Faery Curses

HAUNTS AND HOWLS AND GUARDIAN SPELLS

A CONTEMPORARY FANTASY COLLECTION

KAT SIMONS

CONTENTS

HAUNTS AND HOWLS AND GUARDIAN SPELLS

*To all the lovers of spooky fantasy tales
and heroes toiling to keep the world safe.*

Also, and always, to my family.

INTRODUCTION

My first fiction, the very first stories I wrote as a kid, were all fantasy stories. Make believe worlds full of magic, mystery, and sword-wielding heroes. As I hit my teen years, those stories grew darker—more vampires and ghosts and trouble-making fairies. But still fantasy. Still full of magic and wonder. Even the science fiction I gravitated toward in those impressionable years leaned more toward fantasy—the Dragon Riders of Pern books by Anne McCaffery were seminal for me.

And fantasy is the genre I come back to, again and again, in my writing.

I also come back, again and again, to protector stories. Stories of heroes keeping good guys safe from bad guys. Most of my fiction, fantasy or not, involves a guardian or protector of some kind, a hero making tough decisions to ensure those around them are safe from the dangers of the universe.

That theme moves through so much of my fiction I finally just gave in and wrote an urban fantasy series where I made no bones about what my hero was—Cary Redmond is a

Protector. That's it. That's both her job title and her job description. She saves good guys from bad guys in the most basic of ways, by being a walking, talking shield. She even gets paid for it.

Even beyond that most blatant of setups, I still can't seem to get enough of heroes keeping innocent people safe. So in this collection, I brought together one of my favorite genres with my guardian theme in five never-before-published short stories of fantasy fiction.

Some of the guardians in these pages protect on small levels, some on world-ending levels, all ensuring the balance between dark and light is maintained. In one way or another, each story also involves either some level of haunt, from a cemetery to a pub, or howls, from shapeshifters to legendary beasts.

And of course, because Cary Redmond is my most on-the-nose series, her story involves a nightclub called the Haunt and Howl.

Most of these stories are a little on the darker side—I never did quite get away from my dark paranormal roots—but not so dark they veer into horror. All but one moves from the modern world into a fantasy place of magic and danger, even if that fantasy setting is just beneath the veneer of the mundane realm.

The collection starts in a cemetery, with *Tombstone Wizard*, and a wizard who must confront the evils perpetuated by his former mentor. In *Destiny through the Cat's Eyes*, a secret world opens up for a young historian when she learns her aunt isn't who she's always believed, and neither is she. Then a weary traveler to our realm must find her way home in *Going Out of Business: Everything for Sale*.

The Unshattered Sword is the only story that doesn't move from a contemporary setting into a fantasy world, because it takes place entirely in Faery, but it does give readers a glimpse back into ancient times and the burgeoning start of what will, one day, come to be the Protectors in the Cary Redmond series. When I started writing *The Unshattered Sword*, I had no idea that was the story I was telling until the very end. But there it is, the first spark of what will eventually become the Protectors.

Finally, the collection ends in a nightclub with Cary Redmond herself. *Cary at the Haunt and Howl* takes Cary on an adventure to help her best friend spy on the hinky happenings of a local dance club, only to discover the place is not what it seems.

This volume is filled with a diverse collection of my flights of fantasy, all with guardian heroes at the center of the stories. Two of my favorite things combined into a single collection.

I hope you enjoy reading these short stories, and the dark, dangerous adventures within, as much as I enjoyed writing them.

Kat Simons
September 2021

TOMBSTONE WIZARD

CHAPTER 1

*C*harles settled into his stance at the head of the tombstone, staring out over the graveyard. Rows of elaborate gray and red marble headstones rose in haphazard patters over the hill, interspersed between the maple trees, the grass around them neatly cut. Through the trees, some of the larger family tombs popped over the hill, but in this section of the cemetery, mostly headstones cut into standard arch shapes, only occasionally something more elaborate.

Faintly, the sounds of New York traffic in the distance, but otherwise, the place was silent. The damp air hinted at the rain only a few hours earlier that left muddy puddles along the paved road winding through the graveyard hills. A soft breeze fluttered through the maple leaves, creating a kind of shooshing music.

The cemetery was closed this time of night, the gate locked against visitors until early morning when the caretakers came back and the place opened for business. So he had the quiet darkness to himself.

He only needed an hour. Just an hour to get this done. And then he was sure everything would be okay.

Swallowing hard, he glanced back at the tombstone where he'd set up his gear. The stone was a dark black marble, standing out amongst the gray and red surrounding it, and cut into a miniature obelisk. The base was thick, two steps leading up to the longer obelisk structure. Though only his height, the headstone was nonetheless impressive for standing above the others just next to it. The marble on the obelisk was so highly polished it reflected the moonlight, almost obscuring the name etched into the stone.

He didn't have to see the name to know who's grave this was. He'd been here, during the day, studying the setup, the layout of the cemetery so he could maneuver in the dark without getting lost or tripping and cracking his skull on one of the headstones.

This was the night, and he couldn't afford any mistakes. Not now. Not with the dead bodies piling up.

He had to stop this tonight.

Early in his life, Charlie had thought being a wizard was a thrill, a power that gave him an advantage over the other boys at school, gave him a leg up in the world. That was before he'd met Vincent, before he'd learned what responsibility meant and what real power could actually do. Years ago now, that lesson learned. So long he could barely remember the kid he'd been.

Unfortunately, there were some things he couldn't afford to forget.

He settled onto the damp grass in front of the obelisk to set out his gear. The potions he'd been working on for the last two weeks, all arrayed in neat little bottles in a circle in front of him. The slim blade, just to his right. The ax to his left. Dew seeped through the knees of his jeans, and he shivered, despite his black wool coat. He settled his wool hat down farther over his ears to keep the chill out. While the October night air was cold, the daytime had been warm enough to heat the earth. Already a low ground cover of fog crept through the headstones. He'd hoped that would hold off until much later in the night, after he'd completed his task.

But of course, he wasn't that lucky.

Still, he could manage around the fog. He'd practiced. He knew which bottle held which potion by feel, each little glass vial shaped a little differently with a different type of stopper to keep the potions in. The ax and knife were close enough at hand, he didn't think he'd lose them in the ground fog, but he had alternatives if he did. His ordinary wizard powers, the energy bolts and fire bolts he could summon and use as weapons, wouldn't work against Vincent. Not now. That's why he needed the knife and the ax. But he had enough magic in his bones still, he could use his best weapons if needs be.

Another cold breeze ruffled through the maple leaves overhead, making the moonlight pouring through the branches shiver, casting darkening shadows over the obelisk.

Not much longer now.

A night bird hooted. From the corner of his eye, he saw a dark shadow scramble over the grass toward a tree. His heartbeat started to pound harder so he focused on his breathing, on settling his mind. He and Vincent had avoided this confrontation for a long time. Their time had run out.

The air stilled, Even the nightbirds grew quiet. An unnatural silence dropped over the graveyard. Even the distant traffic sounds vanished. The silence was so complete it was like a sound all its own, blocking out everything, making Charles's ears ring. He swallowed back the fear rising in his throat.

And picked up the knife.

Shadows around the black marble obelisk shifted, despite the lack of air movement. For a long moment, just the shimmering shadow, nothing more. Then from behind the obelisk, a large shape stepped into view.

Vaguely man-shaped, but with a cowl and cloak covering shoulders and head. Taller than Charles by a foot. The area under the cowl too shadowed to show features. Sleeves long enough to cover hands completely. Cloak falling to the wet grass, fully covering legs and feet.

Charles rose slowly, taking one potion bottle and the knife with him as he did.

"You waited a long time," a deep, slightly accented voice from under the cowl. "Is this what you expected?"

"I haven't expected anything at all," Charles said. "Except you."

A chuckle, the sound grating and harsh. "You could have just…stayed away."

"Too many dead." Charles gut clenched at those words. He'd stayed away too long as it was. He should have come sooner. Should have stopped this weeks ago. Preparation had taken him time, and he couldn't have attempted this without that time, but he should have started sooner, the minute the first body appeared.

He'd hoped this wasn't Vincent's work. He'd tried to talk himself out of the truth so he wouldn't have to do this.

"You can't kill a dead man," the being under the cloak said.

"There are other options," Charles said. "Just like death isn't the end. At least not for some."

Another chuckle. "You wouldn't choose this? Immortality. All the power?"

"You're not immortal," Charles said. "Not really. You're dead. You just need to stop coming back."

"When you no longer worry about death," the creature said, "you *are* immortal."

"You could have chosen other options." Charles gestured at the graveyard with the hand holding the knife. "This was a bad one."

The creature pushed the cowl back, revealing himself for the first time. And it took a great deal of willpower, and years of learning and control, for Charles not to react.

There were many things Vincent could have done to achieve his idea of "immortality." He could have become a vampire, allowed himself to be changed, and given himself centuries of life. Life spent mostly in darkness. Life without his sorcerers' skills. That magic didn't often make the jump to vampire, replaced by other skills and strengths. And there was always the possibility that he wouldn't have survived the conversion. Permanent death wasn't uncommon.

Still, it was an option that didn't require others to die. Vampires could live long lives off small amounts of blood. They didn't have to kill to survive. It *had* been an option for Vincent.

There were other ways as well. Though none of the ancient alchemists had discovered the elixir of immortality—and Charles, for his part, was convinced it didn't exist—there were potions, spells, deals with demons, all manner of options to extend a single human life beyond its natural length. Some of those ways came with violence. Some were more mundane.

Vincent had chosen one of the most violent options. He didn't have to. That's the part that Charles couldn't forget. Vincent didn't have to choose this way. He *wanted* this. He had enjoyed violence, death, bloodshed, even before making his transformation. Of course he'd choose the worst possible option for immortality as well.

Blending his soul with an ancient monster, becoming the physical embodiment of that monster…

The first time Vincent had mentioned the possibility, Charles should have known this was where they'd end up.

He should have killed Vincent then.

But he wasn't the murderer between them and never had been. Still, he was here, forced to this point, knowing he was the only one who could stop his former mentor.

And it all sucked. A lot.

Staring up at what had become of his mentor left him sick to his stomach. Blending his essence with the body of the minotaur had left him looking nothing like the Vincent Charles had known. His bull's head, complete with snout and curved horns from his skull, was thick and wider than Vincent's human face had been. There was still a hint of the human Vincent in the shape of the eyes—which glowed red now instead of being simple brown—but everything else was the beast.

The thick, long snout brought his mouth forward, now wide and full of the sharp teeth a real bull wouldn't have. Rough black hair covered his head around the horns, which were long and curved out to the side. His torso was now thickly muscled in a way Vincent had never been, and the same rough black hair on his head grew down his back and across his shoulders. His hands, though still human shaped, were huge now and the very tips of his nails were sharpened to a point. His hooved feet pawed the ground.

While Charles knew this was his former mentor, heard it in the voice, looking at the creature he'd become made it difficult to reconcile the two beings. If the monster hadn't just been talking to him, he wouldn't have been certain this was Vincent.

"You're afraid?" Vincent said. "Disgusted?"

"Sad," Charles said. "I won't ever understand why you did this to yourself."

"Which is why you were left behind when I achieved this."

"You've achieved the ability to kill, taken on a monster and become that monster. I don't see that as an advancement."

"Your vision was always…more narrow and confined than mine."

Given what Charles could do under normal circumstances, he considered that a good thing. Too many beings of power, too many humans born with one kind of magic or another, did horrible things with that power. Charles considered it a responsibility to *not* be one of those people.

"What do you intend to do?" Vincent asked, glancing down at the potions. "You can't stop me. I know what you know. I know your power. None of it is enough to prevent me from completing this transformation."

Charles kept his response to those words to himself, holding Vincent's gaze without reacting, but hearing that the transformation wasn't complete, that there was still time to stop this… Charles hadn't expected that, and the shock of it left him unbalanced. Not a great place to be when he had a job in front of him. Being uncertain in this fight could get him killed.

Still, knowing Vincent wasn't completely lost, hadn't fully integrated the monster yet…

"You want to save me now?" Vincent asked, as if reading his thoughts. His chuckle was deep and echoing and sounded nothing like the man's had sounded when he'd been human. "I don't want to be saved. I've made this deal with the full understanding of what it means. I *embrace this*. What makes you think I'd allow you to ruin everything I've accomplished?"

The fact that Vincent had known where his thoughts went

probably wasn't good. Vincent had just made Charles's job here easier, though. If he refused to be saved, to have the transformation stopped, there really wasn't anything left to save.

"I'm sorry you felt this was the step you had to take," Charles said as he raised the potion he held in one hand. "I'm sorry this obsession has taken you. But I can't allow you to kill anymore."

"Your potions can't kill me," Vincent said as steam blew out of his raised nostrils, filling the cold air.

Fog now covered the grass, obscuring some of Charles's remaining bottles and the ax he'd left there. The white-gray layer of mist crept up the edges of the black obelisk, covering the base, hiding some of the smaller tombstones around them.

Now or never, Charles thought. And he tossed the potion bottle…

Past the minotaur so it smashed into the black marble obelisk.

CHAPTER 2

*V*incent laughed, the sound loud in the dead silent cemetery, echoing off the surrounding maple trees and gravestones, and down through the fog-covered hill. "You missed, boy. A useless potion, now wasted in a bad throw."

The sound of Vincent's deep, beastly chuckle and taunting voice made Charles's teeth clench. But he kept his own attention on the effects of his potion, ignoring the monster that was his former mentor as best he could.

A heartbeat of worry, of fear, clenched Charles's chest as he waited. He knew this would take time, but still, the waiting let in uncertainty, let in the waffling terror that he'd failed.

Then the obelisk seemed to pulse, the black marble stretching and snapping back to its original shape. And then, with a suddenness that had Charles nearly stepping backward, the obelisk grew, lengthened, shot up to tower over them both, rising through the maple leaves fast enough to leave the scent of maple sap in its wake.

Vincent snarled and looked up at the growing stone. "What have you done?"

Charles didn't answer. He picked up the next potion bottle and tossed it at the now huge obelisk.

This time Vincent stretched out a monstrously large hand and tried to grab the bottle before it hit marble. But Charles feinted forward with his knife, slicing at Vincent and forcing him back a step, even though they both knew in this realm that knife would do little against a minotaur.

The bottle connected with the obelisk in a shriek of shattered glass and spraying liquid. This potion was clear colored, so it looked merely like water had splashed against the stone.

A deceptive visual.

"What have you done?" the monster roared.

A sound so loud it hurt Charles's ears. He ignored the pain and tossed the final potion needed for this part of the incantation. It shattered against the obelisk, releasing a hiss of steam and the scent of dust and olives as it mixed with the other potion. Then he poured some of his own magic into a chant that would release the spell.

"No!"

Vincent's scream came too late. Around them, the ground heaved, the earth trembled, and stones rose high above them, encircling them, growing from the mist until they blocked out the night sky.

Once the circling stones were taller than the obelisk, more stone formed a roof overhead, slapping down on the walls with a thunderous thud. Charles did wince at the sound, now louder and echoing as they were cut off from the natural world, encased, entombed...

"What have you done?" Vincent screamed again.

"Returned the monster to where it belongs," Charles said.

As the labyrinth grew around them.

The stones moved and shifted, even as the ceiling sealed

overhead, plunging them into darkness. Charles called a small ball of blue energy onto his palm. Even at its strongest, the wizard bolt wouldn't be able to damage the immortal minotaur, but it lit the overwhelming darkness just fine.

"This won't stop me," Vincent said.

"We'll see."

The walls curved around the obelisk, then, moving in between him in Vincent, separating them.

Vincent's roar of anger echoed through the twists of the growing labyrinth. It was no longer the sound of an outraged human, but the beastly roar of a wild animal.

Fog continued to cover the floor, leaving it impossible to see, but underfoot felt more solid now, like stone instead of grass.

Charles pushed the knife he still held into the scabbard tucked into his belt. Then carefully, one at a time, he settled the remaining two potion bottles into the inner pocket of his coat, maneuvering them with one hand while holding the wizard bolt up high to keep his surroundings illuminated. He hadn't thought the forming labyrinth would separate him from Vincent. But it was just as well. That was the point wasn't it. Find the center of the maze and kill the monster.

Not that he could kill the minotaur. And he hadn't intended to try. He'd intended to lose the monster inside the maze and make his own way out of the labyrinth.

His original plan was to trap Vincent and the minotaur here, in the labyrinth, where the monster belonged. Once Charles found his way out, he could seal the entrance, and ensure Vincent remained trapped and harmless in his immortality. Charles still intended to do that to the minotaur.

But now that he knew he could break the bond Vincent had made with the monster, he felt obligated to try. Even if

Vincent didn't want that separation. Even if he *wanted* to remain the beast.

Leaving the minotaur and Vincent bonded here, even sealed in, meant that the wizard might one day find a way out. Being able to separate them, and leave the beast sealed in the labyrinth, ensured it, at least, was trapped for eternity and unable to cause harm because it wouldn't have the intelligence and cunning of an evil human who could wield magic to help it escape.

Unfortunately, since that hadn't been part of the original plan, he wasn't sure how to do it.

Once he had the remaining glass bottles of potion inside his coat, he reached into the fog for the ax. It wasn't an ordinary ax. He'd worked hard to ensure it wasn't ordinary. That had taken more time, extra magic, time that might have cost more lives. But he couldn't have faced the minotaur without it. The steel, double-headed blades were now infused with enough magic to wound the immortal beast. And since they were trapped together inside the labyrinth now, that ability to wound the creature tracking him would come in handy.

He turned in a slow circle, fully taking in his surroundings finally. The ceiling overhead had circular patterns cut into the red-brown stone, interspersed with little starburst, making it look like a stylized night sky. The walls were bare stone, no markings to indicate where he was inside the maze or which direction to go. The obelisk was the center. The maze moved out from there. But even if he moved through the dark and found the center, that wouldn't get him to the entrance.

He had, however, ensured he'd have a string.

Another roar of beastly anger echoed through the corridors. No telling where the beast was now. A creeping tension crawled through Charles's gut. He'd have preferred the labyrinth hadn't separated him from Vincent, even if that was the maze's whole point. He'd have preferred to know exactly where Vincent was initially. He knew this wouldn't be easy. It wasn't supposed to be. But the tension of not knowing where the monster was and waiting for it to move out of the shadows left his muscles tight and his nerves jumping.

Taking a deep breath, he tossed the wizard bolt in one random direction, watching it recede into the darkness, taking his only source of light with it. It didn't slam into any monsters. Hopefully, that was a good sign. Without the wizard bolt, the blackness engulfed him. No light leaked through the stone ceiling. He stepped close to the wall, feeling his way in the dark until his fingers touched stone. The walls were roughhewn but dry.

Now that he couldn't see anything, the scents inside the labyrinth made themselves more obvious, a strangely dusty smell that seemed to be tinged with some sort of spice he couldn't identify clearly, something earthy like oregano maybe. It wasn't a bad smell, and for some reason, that surprised him. He'd expected dank and moldy and stale. The fog covering the floor had only enforced that expectation. So dry and herby were disorienting.

Maybe that was the point? The maze was intended to disorient and confuse. Mixing up the senses with different impressions assaulting each sense was definitely disorienting.

Ignoring the damp feeling around his legs and the way it conflicted with the dry walls and herb-laced smell of the corridor, Charles focused on the core of his own magic, sending a pulse of power into the stone, hunting for the "string" he'd worked into his potions.

There. The line in the stones, touched and activated by his magic. He blinked and realized he'd closed his eyes even though in the darkness he didn't need to. Even with his eyes open, he couldn't see anything. The "string" didn't light up to show the way. But he could feel the line now.

He started following it in one direction and felt a shock vibrate through his fingertips. Grunting, he moved in the opposite direction. This time a tingle traveled through his fingers, a pleasant, almost eager sensation.

Okay. Pleasant vibration meant he was heading in the right direction. Shock meant he'd turned the wrong way.

He could do this. He could.

Letting out a slow breath, he followed the line, his fingers firm against the wall as he shuffled through the darkness, keeping his feet low to the ground, pushing forward instead of taking large steps so he could ensure he didn't trip over anything. He didn't dare light up the corridor with another wizard bolt and risk giving himself away to the minotaur. But knowing the creature was out there, stalking through the maze, hunting for him, was as nerve wracking and terrifying as he'd feared.

Sweat dripped down his temples and back, making his heavy coat feel uncomfortably warm. The air moved, a faint breeze from somewhere, but only barely, and compared to the cold cemetery, the labyrinth was sweltering. Over the herb and dust scents surrounding him, he could smell his own sweat now, his fear too strong to contain.

Damn it. That wasn't good.

The minotaur could track him through smell.

Charles picked up speed, still trying to shuffle so he didn't trip over anything while moving faster along the magical string.

In the blackness, without his sight to rely on, his sense of hearing and touch were heightened, and the sounds of shifting dirt, groaning rocks, the occasional pebble kicked over the stone floor, all of it amplified, a giant booming cascade of noise that would alert the minotaur to his presence. Each scraping step forward pierced his skull, had his jaw tight as he winced and tried to hold his concentration.

The string to the entrance was, like a real string, something he could drop if he lost focus for too long. He'd have to pause and find it again if he let it go. And all of that would cost him time he didn't have.

Every moment inside the maze gave the minotaur time to find him.

Charles edged along the wall as fast as he dared, his fingers skimming rough rock, holding the magical connection to his string by will, the ax in his other hand heavy, the scents of herby dust and his own sweat filling the darkness around him.

He had no doubt Vincent was looking for him, looking for the way out. The wizard would know this was an eternal prison if he didn't reach Charles before Charles escaped. And with every step, every bump of his fingers on the rough stone wall, every breath that wheezed out of him, Charles felt the tick of time and the approach of disaster.

His shoulders hunched under the weight of fear. He could practically feel something creeping through the blackness behind him.

But Vincent wouldn't feel the need to hide his presence, would he. He'd have light. He'd use a spell and give himself a way to see through the encompassing darkness. And that light would alert Charles to his location. He'd be warned. He'd know the minotaur was approaching.

At least, he hoped that's what Vincent would do. The

minotaur couldn't see in the blackness any better than Charles could, despite this being the beast's destined home. There was no light here for even the best night vision to use. Everything Charles had read confirmed the minotaur wouldn't have that advantage here.

Still, the worry that he'd missed something, that he was wrong and somehow the blending of Vincent with the minotaur had given them skills they hadn't had before, that worry had his hackles up and his tension high. His shoulders were so tight they ached. And he could swear he felt the breath of the beast on his neck.

He paused, listening, straining for sound and smell. Still only his own sweat and the faintly herb and dust blend of the surroundings. The quiet, when he held his breath and didn't move, was overwhelming. His ears actually rang with the sheer silence of it.

The journey out of the maze was part of this spell. A necessary part of the process of trapping the minotaur. He had to do this or the spell wouldn't take, the labyrinth wouldn't imprison the beast. Everything he'd read and studied had agreed. There were ways to make the journey out easier. The string leading him back to the entrance was absolutely necessary. But the journey had to be made. The challenge had to be faced. Without this, the spell crumbled. And Charles would be right back where he'd started with a dangerous wizard inhabiting the minotaur, on the loose in his world, killing to ensure the wizard's immortality.

He couldn't let his former mentor win this. Vincent was too dangerous. And too smart. If Charles failed this time, he'd never have another chance. Even if he survived.

Though in this case, failing would likely mean his death.

He was less afraid of the death than the failure.

He pushed forward, dragging his feet over the stone while

trying to keep quiet, holding his breath and letting it out in long slow exhales so he wouldn't hyperventilate. All the while listening. Listening through the ringing silence for the approaching monster.

The drawing tension made him want to scream, to shout into the silence and break the standoff. He kept his mouth tightly closed, but the roar of overwhelming fear and tension climbed up his throat.

Vincent had taught him to control those emotions. Fear for a wizard could be deadly. Controlling emotions when working with his inner magic had required years of practice and training. And he'd been a good student. He was a very good wizard.

The problem was he had never outstripped his master. Vincent had always been better.

The only real advantage Charles had, was that he'd surprised Vincent with this conjuring. But now that they were trapped together, Charles's advantage was significantly depleted. Only the thin magical string imbedded in the wall and his bespelled ax.

His fingers skimmed over the rough stone, rubbing his fingertips like sandpaper. The string was securely in his hold at the moment, his magical connection to that lifeline solid. But with every step, every scrape of his fingers over the stone, the pain of that constant rub made itself known. He must have cut himself somewhere on the journey, because the ache turned to pain. He didn't dare take his fingers off the wall and lose his connection with the string, but if he was bleeding…

He was leaving a trail for the minotaur to follow.

Even more than the stink of his fear-induced sweat, a trail of blood would call the beast.

He had to hurry.

The ax in his right had grew heavier with each step, but the weight of it was some comfort as well. Having a weapon against the beast, even if he couldn't kill it, gave him a measure of…well not security precisely, but a sense that he wouldn't necessarily die immediately. There was something to that.

A sound, distant and echoing through the twisting corridors brought him up short.

A roar.

The minotaur.

But the sound bounced off walls and through curves and dead ends making it impossible to place the monster's location. Still, the sound, the announcement of its presence, had Charles's adrenaline spiking, his fear ratcheting up until he was panting.

He pushed forward, his only option, but the sense of approaching doom danced along his spine and up his neck.

He could feel the slickness of blood from his fingertips over the stone now. A too-easy-to-follow trail. But he couldn't stop. And he couldn't take his fingers away from the stone to stop the bleeding. To lose the connection with his lifeline now, when the monster had announced its pursuit so blatantly, would be deadly.

Another roar, followed by Vincent's deep voice. "I'm coming, Charles. You can't escape me. I will rip your head off and drink your blood before crumbling this creation of yours to the ground."

Charles tightened his grip on the ax as he pushed forward. Remaining silent felt impossible. He wanted to shout back and break into a run. He wanted to scream denials. And he wanted to race forward so badly it took effort to keep his steps purposeful and measured. Rushing wouldn't help him. Though the flight instinct was strong, running when he couldn't see anything, when his only solid connection to the path out was through his now bleeding fingertips, could get him killed.

He reined in the instinct, but it took will. And it wasn't easy.

Another roar in the darkness, this one sounding closer. It was impossible to tell, though. Sound bounced around him like a rubber ball. No way to trace either distance or location of the starting point. No way to know which direction the sound actually came from.

He sucked in lungfuls of air, filling his mouth with the dusty flavor of whatever herb scented the labyrinth and the bitter musk of his own sweat. He had no way of knowing how much farther he had to go.

Only that he had to keep going.

"I can smell you, Charles," the voice through the darkness echoed and taunted.

Charles tried not to pant, tried to keep his breathing even. It took more willpower not to conjure a wizard bolt, for light and protection. It took effort not to scream. Not to say anything at all. His heartbeat pounded so hard he was sure the minotaur could hear that as well as smell the fear pumping off him.

He had to reach the end. He had to find his way out and seal the labyrinth. He didn't dare let the creature out again. But if the minotaur killed him inside the labyrinth, the spell broke apart. The labyrinth crumbled. And no one would stand in Vincent's way.

Charles couldn't let that happen.

He hefted his ax, adjusting the weight and balance as he continued running his blood-slicked, stinging fingers along the rough wall.

Had the maze not cut him off from Vincent initially, he

might have been able to incapacitate the minotaur from the start, used the ax to wound the creature long enough to make this escape without being stalked.

But that wasn't the price, wasn't the challenge, was it? That would have made this too easy. It wasn't supposed to be easy.

A breeze brushed his hair where it stuck to his temples, cool and ominous. The air was fresh, it moved enough not to taste stale. But there hadn't been a breeze before this. He wanted to stop, wanted to swing out with his ax. Every hair on his body rose. Tension coiled in his gut. A scream climbed up his throat. A roar of denial crowding that scream.

Whispers carried through the tunnel now, whispers in Greek. Vincent didn't speak Greek, but the minotaur did. Charles only had enough knowledge to have established the spell. He'd worked through translations and a passing knowledge of Latin to get here. And then all of it written, not spoken. The words floating around him in the darkness were incomprehensible to him.

But the threat seemed obvious.

Whether it was a conjuring or another kind of spell from Vincent, whether the words were just whispered threats, or whether they carried power, Charles couldn't tell. They could be the ghosts of all those who'd died in the labyrinth for all he knew. But the source of the threatening taunting hushed moans hardly mattered.

He had to reach the entrance. That was his only hope.

Another breeze brushed past him, carrying a faint musky animal scent.

It took everything in him not to startle from the breeze. His imagination created images to taunt him—the minotaur standing only a few feet away in the darkness; the minotaur breathing on him, purposefully taunting to increase Charles's fear; the minotaur about to strike. Vincent had a physical weapon but also magic. And while Charles's energy bolts wouldn't work against the minotaur, Vincent's would work against Charles.

But did Vincent still have access to those inherently wizard skills now that he was the minotaur? None of Charles's reading had been clear on whether or not the human blending its essence with the immortal beast would retain its human magical skills. Some authors had said yes, others no. He'd been hoping for the no.

But in the pitch blackness, feeling his way along the wall, the ominous breeze brushing his face as he stumbled forward, he feared the answer was yes.

His boot connected with a rock as he slid his foot forward and the rock skittered across the stone floor, the sound of the clink clink like the boom of thunder echoing in the tunnels. The whispers stopped.

Damn it. Had he given himself away? Maybe Vincent hadn't found him yet.

He pushed as fast as he could, moving at a near trot now without losing contact with the walls and his magical lifeline.

Another musky breeze brushed his temples and a cold shiver raced down his spine.

Entrance? Or beast?

Impossible to tell.

He gave up attempting to be silent. Between his bleeding fingers leaving a visible trail and the stink of his sweat and blood, the beast would track him soon, with or without light to see by. Charles had to hurry. The tingling sensation of the string shivered pleasantly and curved in a direction that Charles followed at a near run. The sense of eagerness increased as he went, as if the string was telling him he was almost there, almost to his destination.

Almost to the end of the maze.

Rushing headlong into the dark wasn't his smartest move, but he didn't care. He had to get out, to finish this, before the minotaur caught him. He bumped against the wall as he worked to keep his fingers in contact with the string. The ax weighed heavily and awkwardly in his other hand and he bounced it a few times to better his grip. All while jogging faster and faster.

Coming around a sharp corner, nearly tripping over himself as he ran through the blackness, Charles came to an abrupt halt as torch light suddenly flared, dazzling his eyes painfully. He raised the hand with the ax, blocking his eyes with his arm in a delayed and pointless attempt to keep the glaring light from overwhelming him.

He squinted in the sudden light, his eyes slowly adjusting to being able to see again, even as the scent of smoke from the flaming torch scent a panicked pulse of terror through him. Not terror of the smoke, of fire ripping through the maze, though there was a primitive element of that under his more dominant fear.

Terror. Horror.

As he looked past his arm.

At the black, tombstone obelisk at the very center of the labyrinth.

CHAPTER 4

Charles almost dropped the ax, very nearly dropped to his knees, as defeat washed over him.

The obelisk again. The center of the labyrinth.

The opposite of direction he'd meant to go.

He wasn't near the entrance. He wasn't almost out. He was right back at the very center of the maze. Looking at the black marble of the grown and expanded obelisk that had marked Vincent's "grave" in the cemetery.

He'd failed.

Somehow, the magical string he'd left himself to escape the labyrinth had led him in the wrong direction. Or maybe Vincent had somehow found and altered the string so that it led Charles back here.

Either way, he was no longer heading out of the maze. He was right back at the very heart of it. Staring in the torch light. Overwhelmed by the stench of smoke from the torch's fire as well as the stink of his own failure.

While Vincent stood next to the obelisk. Laughing.

The tone and depth of the noise coming from the beast

wasn't Vincent's. Too deep and guttural. The minotaur's voice. But Vincent's mocking. Vincent's triumph.

"You think you can beat me, boy?" Vincent asked. "I've had years to prepare for this. You don't think I'd know the one thing that could stop me. And how to counter it?"

Charles didn't answer. What could he say? No, he hadn't thought Vincent would know how to get out of this labyrinth. Not like this. By leading Charles back to the center again. He'd expected a fight. Excepted Vincent to hunt him through the maze. Expected Vincent to try and stop him.

But he hadn't expected they'd both end up right back at the center, in front of Vincent's tombstone.

For the first time since finding the magical string he'd implanted in the labyrinth walls, Charles dropped that line he'd thought was leading him toward the entrance. Pointless now. The spell pulsed with eagerness, with a sense that he had "arrived" at his destination.

He'd arrived at the end alright. Just not the end he'd been aiming for.

He let out a long breath as failure swamped him. He had no backup plan, no alternate course. There was no way to find a path through the maze without that string to lead him. He could dive back into the blackness, attempt to find a way out without the string. But he would fail. Or more likely just be killed by the minotaur before he got anywhere near the entrance. Hell, Vincent could leave him to wander around the maze until he starved to death if he really wanted to torture Charles.

And once Charles died, the prison of the labyrinth would crumble and release Vincent and the minotaur onto the world again.

"Don't you know, boy," Vincent said, "The minotaur has

to be killed before you can escape the labyrinth. You can't skip that step and get out."

"That's not the prison I called," Charles murmured, pointlessly. They both knew the minotaur couldn't actually be killed. The magic Charles had worked here wasn't supposed to be contingent on killing the beast. But he didn't have the energy or will to argue with Vincent. Or himself for that matter.

He'd tried. He'd failed.

More innocent people would die now. And there was nothing he could do about it.

He stared at the bull's head on top of wide, human shoulders. Barely anything of Vincent there. Steam snorted from the beast's nose, joining the smoke from the torch fire, and the thin layer of mist that covered the stone floor. Even the faint scent of herbs was gone now. Leaving only the stench of smoke and beast and sweat.

"Shall I kill you fast?" Vincent asked. "Or slowly?"

Charles let out a snort of a laugh, a defeated chuff that had nothing to do with amusement and everything to do with the pointlessness of his attempt to stop his former mentor. He'd been arrogant, to think he could win. Arrogant to think he could take Vincent this easily.

He stared at the blood slicking his hand, some of it dried and caking under his nails, some of it still leaking out of the multiple cuts and abrasions scrapped into his fingertips. He had required some of his own blood to make this conjuring work, to meld the magic he called with his internal magic and bring forward this labyrinth. His potions had required those drops of blood to catalyze the process. And he'd given the blood willingly to make this happen.

He was still giving blood to the labyrinth, he thought with

a hint of ironic humor that was closer to hysteria. He'd left a trail of blood in his wake.

If only that trail had led to the entrance and not right back to the center of his own destruction.

"Slowly?" Vincent asked again. "Or quick?"

Charles waved his bloody hand in disinterest. He knew Vincent had already chosen what he wanted to do, and nothing Charles said now would change that.

He'd fight. Because he couldn't just stand here and let Vincent kill him without at least fighting back. But he couldn't kill the minotaur. Which meant, eventually, Charles would die.

The memory of Vincent's words in the graveyard came to him, that Vincent and minotaur weren't fully bonded yet. That they needed more death before this bargain was sealed and Vincent became permanently entwined with the immortal beast.

Was there… Could there be a weakness there? Something he could exploit to actually kill the beast? Or maybe just separate Vincent from the beast. Not to save Vincent. That wasn't possible. But maybe that would be enough to distract them both, to give Charles time to find a way out of the labyrinth.

He knew the blending of the two had taken a great deal of magic to begin with, maybe most of what Vincent had at his disposal. Even if Charles knew how to separate them, he wasn't sure he had enough of his own reserves of magic to accomplish the task. He'd used too much just to create the labyrinth, to build the prison. And he still didn't know *how* to pull his former mentor from this symbiotic blending with the minotaur.

He considered the ax, the spells worked into the pointed

steel. He couldn't kill the beast with it, but he'd brought it in case he had to wound the minotaur. Would wounding the minotaur weaken the bond between it and Vincent? Would wounding it give Charles time to find his way out of this mess? Or just make the creature angrier and more vicious?

Did any of that matter now?

He hefted the ax, wrapping his second hand around the handle, letting his blood sink into the smooth wood.

"A fight?" Vincent chuckled. He set the torch into a hole in the floor, hidden by the mist, but enough to keep the torch upright and lighting the chamber. Shadows of flickering orange light danced over the black marble obelisk like spirits anticipating the battle.

Vincent stalked toward him, rolling his massive shoulders, steam puffing from his thick bull's nose. He'd dropped the cowl and hood at some point, so the minotaur stood in all his monstrous glory, leather pants covering his lower body, his massive chest glistening faintly with sweat in the warm air, his hooved feet clonking against the stone floor as he approached.

Charles lifted the ax, letting it rest over one shoulder. He'd never been a physical fighter, at least not much of one. Neither had Vincent. The minotaur, on the other hand, was made to kill.

Snorting softly in the otherwise quiet room, Vincent smiled. Then charged with his head lowered, pointed horns aimed for Charles.

Stepping to one side and ducking to avoid the horns of the much larger creature, Charles swung his ax at the creature's side. Vincent knocked the ax away like it was an annoying fly, and the momentum shift sent Charles stumbling backward into a wall. He dove aside just as Vincent charged again.

Vincent slammed head first into the wall, so hard the sound echoed and the structure shivered. Dust showered down from the ceiling, settling on Vincent's huge, hairy shoulders.

He spun, seemingly unaffected by having just bashed his head against a stone wall, and charged at Charles again.

Another dive to one side, awkward with the heavy ax in hand. Charles swung again, this time aiming for the minotaur's leg. The ax connected, though not well, but enough to slice across the monster's thigh. Vincent roared and reached for the ax. Charles jerked it away and danced backward. If Vincent got the ax from him, he'd be defenseless. All his magic, all his powers, meant nothing against the minotaur.

Not unless he could figure out a way to separate his former mentor from the monster.

But how?

The chamber around the obelisk was open, a circular room marking the center of the maze, and that the obelisk tombstone was the only thing in the room. Charles dove behind its cover, putting it between he and Vincent, hoping for some breathing room. His wounded hand stung and blood dripped from his fingertips still, slicking the wooden ax handle. If Vincent got a hold on the ax, he'd be able to pull it free easily. Even if Charles had the strength to hold it against the minotaur, the blood had made his grip on the handle uncertain at best.

The remaining potion in his inner coat pocket knocked against his ribs, reminding him of the plan, to trap Vincent inside. He'd assumed reaching the entrance and sealing that with the potion would be the end. But what if…

What if he just sealed the labyrinth? Right here. At its center. At the obelisk? He'd be trapped. And he'd die. But

Vincent could leave once the prison was sealed, and that would save hundreds of lives.

"You can't win," Vincent said as he stomped the floor, scraping the stone with one hoof, loud enough Charles winced. "I will kill you. And I'll escape."

"You might kill me," Charles murmured, "but you won't escape."

He looked up at the obelisk, the back smooth and unadorned. No markings or carvings to mar the perfectly polished black stone. Vincent used this obelisk, this tombstone, to mark a death he would never have. But he also used it to hide. The minotaur's home when it wasn't out killing. The place the creature rested in between hunts. That was why it was at the center of the labyrinth, why Charles was able to use it to build the maze. It was the creature's dwelling.

Did that mean there was a way back out through the obelisk?

That…wasn't good. It meant his plan had had this flaw worked into it the entire time. Could Vincent leave through the obelisk even if Charles had succeeded in sealing the labyrinth entrance?

Before he had time to consider that possibility more, the monster dove around the barrier, reaching for him. Charles dropped into the mist from the low base of the obelisk, scrambling to put distance between himself and Vincent, the ax sliding from his hands when he slammed into the ground.

Stupid. He'd stopped paying attention to where Vincent was inside the room. And the only reason the minotaur hadn't just ripped his head off was because Vincent wanted to play with him.

He wasn't going to win this in a physical fight. Not

against the minotaur. But he could win. He just needed a little time to work the final spell, to finish this and seal the labyrinth shut for all time.

He pushed to his feet and swiped up the ax as Vincent laughed.

"You'll make a good meal," he said. "And when I've feasted on you, I'll sleep. Then I'll finish what I've started. You can't stop me, Charles."

Instead of backing away, as he'd been doing, giving ground and waiting for the minotaur to attack, Charles hefted the ax and roared, a sound of defiance so loud it bounced off the walls and ceiling. He charged, the ax raised over his head.

The attack was sudden enough, and out of character enough, that Vincent balked and took a step back. The hesitance, the surprise, gave Charles an opening, small and brief, but an opening. He swung the ax in a wide arc and buried it into the side of the monster's neck.

Even his magical ax couldn't remove the minotaur's head. But the weapon still buried deep enough in the side of the creature's throat to hurt it. Vincent stumbled backward, the ax still buried deep, scrambling at it as blood poured down his chest.

Charles turned back to the obelisk, taking the remaining potions from his coat. His skin crawled, knowing the minotaur would free the ax soon. The sounds of Vincent's tight-lipped grunts and guttural sounds of anger set Charles's teeth on edge.

He murmured the catalyst spell that would activate the potions and then tossed both bottles at the obelisk.

Without waiting to see if it worked, he spun back to the monster and charged again, scrambling with it to take back the ax, using the knife from his belt scabbard to stab at the creature's arm as he tried to pull the ax free.

He was no match for the monster's strength, though. Vincent batted him aside like an annoying pup, sending Charles flying into the obelisk…

And through it. Onto the damp grass in the cemetery.

CHAPTER 5

Charles blinked at his surroundings, the dark night and fresh cold air chilling the sweat on his brow, the grass wet under his jeans. He'd landed on his ass, his back up against another tombstone, looking up at the obelisk as it was in this realm, smaller and lit by moonlight instead of torchlight. The smell of grass and maple trees overwhelmed the stink of his own fear.

A roar, sounding distant but too close from inside the obelisk.

Charles scrambled to his feet. His knife and ax were still inside the labyrinth with Vincent, so he called up a wizard bolt, even knowing the spherical ball of blue electrical energy would do nothing against the monster.

The opening between the labyrinth and Charles's world was still open, since he'd just gone through it. His sealing potions must not have worked?

He approached the obelisk slowly, carefully, waiting for the moment the minotaur stepped out, his brain too overwhelmed by the failure of his last spell to think clearly.

He had to find a way to keep the creature inside the labyrinth, but he couldn't think. Too much panic had sucked out his logic.

A thick, long hand reached through the black marble. Another roar echoing into his world from a distance. Charles raised his bolt, ready to throw it, some half-formed idea that he could force the monster back into the labyrinth and try again to seal the opening. Even though he had no more potions or spells ready to do that. No other way to trap the beast.

But as he watched the hand reaching through the stone, stretching forward, palm up, it started to change color. From the wrist, rising to the fingertips, the beast's hair covered skin paled to an almost gray color, solidifying as the color moved across the palm. The very tips of the fingers flexed and then were covered by the gray.

Freezing the hand in place.

Another roar from deep inside the obelisk.

The sound cut off abruptly, leaving the cemetery silent as the hand sticking out of the obelisk darkened to a black marble.

Charles blinked a few times, frowning, not quite believing what he saw.

The minotaur's hand, now an immobile piece of stone, polished black like the surrounding marble, stuck out from the center of the obelisk, on the smooth side which hadn't had any writing on it. Now, around the large, reaching hand, etched into the stone, was an intricate, circular maze drawing, a miniaturized picture of the labyrinth, with the creature's hand marking the very center.

Charles moved closer, slowly, still holding the wizard bolt on his palm.

No more herb-scented dust, just wet grass and maple leaves. No more faint breeze in air that shouldn't have been moving. Now a stronger, cold wind whistled between the tombstones. The only sounds, night birds and the distant sound of traffic on the main road just outside of the far side of the graveyard.

By the blue light of his wizard bolt, Charles watched a flickering shimmer of electrical sparks circle through the maze drawing, running along the lines of the image in a streak of blue lightning.

And then even that settled.

Leaving behind a strange and morbid feature at the back of the obelisk tombstone.

Despite his better instincts, Charles still reached up and touched the stone hand. He flinched away almost instantly, anticipating movement, worrying about the monster grabbing him.

But nothing happened. And the stone had felt cold, solid, and…not living.

He wobbled a little as the adrenaline left him shaky. Closing his hand to reabsorb the wizard bolt, he sunk to his knees in the wet grass, letting the cold air wrap around him.

He watched the stone hand. He wasn't sure how long. Minutes? Hours? But he watched it. Waiting for movement. Waiting for…something.

The sky started to lighten. Not dawn yet, but close. Approaching. The wind died down. The chilled air bit into his exposed hands and face, leaving him shivering and sore from remaining on his knees on the damp ground for so long. No mist covered the grass now, but the feel of the approaching dawn left him sure the mist would roll in again as the sun rose.

The cemetery caretakers would arrive soon. The neighborhood waking up as another work day started. He had to leave.

Still, he waited for the first bright spark of sunlight to touch the obelisk, assuring himself the minotaur was well and truly trapped, before he climbed, creaking and groaning, back to his feet. He stretched his back muscles, wincing as his joints protested his vigil, even as he continued to stare at the stone hand circled by the stylized maze sticking out of the obelisk.

He thought back through the sealing spell used to make the last potions. He'd have to do some research, make sure this was an end. But instinct told him this was done. The potions, though not working as he'd planned, had worked. Trapped the monster. Inside the labyrinth.

At least for as long as the obelisk tombstone stood.

He made his way slowly through the cemetery to an area of chainlink fence he'd be able to climb to get back out, trying not to think of what it meant that the hand had been trapped, what that meant for the creature on the other side of that hand. A creature that couldn't die.

Some things were too horrible to contemplate.

But the monster wouldn't keep killing. And that was, as far as Charles was concerned, a win.

He glanced back through the fence, past the climbing ivy that partially blocked the view of the cemetery hill where the obelisk sat between other, more conventional gravestones.

He'd return tonight. And the next night. Just to make sure the trap had taken. Just to make sure the monster couldn't escape. He'd watch the news closely, for signs of new, unexplained deaths that might mean the monster was back in this realm. He'd research the possible reactions of the potions he'd used to do this and make sure this had really worked.

But for now…

He was alive. The monster was trapped. No one else would die.

Yeah. He'd definitely count that as a win.

GOING OUT OF BUSINESS: EVERYTHING'S FOR SALE

CHAPTER 1

Teri climbed out of her non-descript gray Corolla, from the freezing air conditioning into the dust dry heat of the Las Vegas summertime, and groaned, stretching her back muscles. The change felt delicious, the heat a satisfying warmth on her skin after the car's cold interior, but she knew that heat would sap and drain her in a few minutes. At least it was dry and not humid. She hated hot humidity.

The creosote smell of the desert was getting old, though, and she could do without the background taste of all that dust. Time for some cooler climates.

Past time.

She stared at the strip mall in front of her, a long row of stores anchored at one end by a drug store and at the other by a liquor store. All the businesses in between were pretty ordinary looking. A dollar store. A cheap clothing shop. A hole-in-the-wall burger joint that didn't look the most appetizing. A coffee place that did look nice enough to enter. There was a discrete porn shop tucked up next to the liquor store, a pet shop next to the drug store. And right in the middle of it all, a place with boarded up windows and a sign on a large banner over the door.

Going Out of Business! Everything's on Sale!

That would be the place.

At least, she hoped she'd finally gotten it right. She'd been searching half the United States Southwest for this particular store. She was a little surprised how many strip malls there were in this country. And how many had signs that proclaimed they were going out of business and had to sell everything. Although, what surprised her more about that was just how long those "going out of business" stores had been open. The last one she'd tried had been "going out of business" for over three years.

The parking lot was mostly empty. Three cars were parked in front of the drug store and two in front of the liquor store, but most of the central lot was open black tarmac. She'd parked her car in the middle and near the back part of the lot, next to the relatively quiet street just off the I15 heading out of town, back toward California. Heat waved up off the tarmac between her and the stores, creating eddies of shimmering air. That same heat that had felt lovely on her skin just a moment earlier now had her sweating through her t-shirt and regretting her jeans.

She shielded her eyes from the sun with one hand and stared at the store with the boarded up windows. This had to be the place. She'd spent months trying to find it. This had to be the place.

She reached into the car and pulled her muted green backpack off the passenger seat, dropping it carefully over one shoulder. The car door slamming shut sounded loud in the empty lot. Pressing the button on her key fob to lock her door, letting the little beep beep of the alarm reassure her the car would still be here when she returned—if she returned—

she headed toward the store with the boarded up windows, checking her surroundings as she went. There weren't any people. Just the five cars spread across the lot. A bedraggled black and white cat slunk across the sidewalk near the drug store, disappearing around the corner. Other than that sign of life, the place felt deserted.

The eaves over the sidewalk in front of the stores provided minimal shade this time of day, the sun angle keeping the white walkway baking and radiating heat up through the soles of her cheap tennis shoes. She checked one last time over her shoulder. No people around, no one driving into the lot, no one passing on the empty sidewalk. The desert across from the strip mall was an empty landscape of dirt and rock. In the distance she could just see a 7-11 and a few scattered houses. Beyond that, a line of purple mountains. That was it. No one around.

She flexed her fingers once, as her hand hovered over the door handle to the "Going out of business" store. If this wasn't the right place…

With a quiet curse, she pushed at the swinging glass door.

A blast of cool, humid air hit her in the face. She sighed and stepped inside, closing the door behind her.

*P*lunging into the dark coolness after the bright heat outside forced Teri to pause just inside the door and let her eyes adjust. The dark overhead wooden beams gave the room a cozy feeling, though they were tall enough to not leave the place feeling short and claustrophobic. The scuffed wooden floor was clean, with a scattering of sweet-smelling straw under the nearest tables. The rounded windows behind her let in soft gray light, like a rainstorm had kicked up outside. And the overhead lamps flickered with firelight.

She pulled in a deep, satisfied breath. The place smelled of meat pasties, *good* beer, and the slightly funky undertone of the trolls sitting near the front of the pub.

She glanced their way. Two of them, leaning over the round wooden table they made look small, their huge, hairless heads close as they talked around mouthfuls of meat pies. Their leather pants and jerkins over huge, hairless gray bodies looked sweltering after the desert heat, but given the temperature inside the pub, she had to assume they were comfortable. They had two ceramic flagons of beer between them, and their conversation looked intense, but was too quiet for her to eavesdrop.

Across from the door, a demon and an elf stared at a chessboard set up on the table between them. Well, the elf stared at the chessboard. The demon was staring at the elf, and her smile was smug. She lounged back in the wooden, low backed chair, one arm draped over the back. Her black silk suit jacket gaping wide across her pale chest, her short black hair cut into a bob that framed a demonically sexy face —because of course it did. She had a huge double headed ax leaning against the wall behind her chair, the wrist-thick handle twinned in silver.

Her chess counterpart scowled at the board, his features sharp and elegant, his pointed ears peeking out from his long blond hair. He was dressed in green dress slacks and a long sleeved, button down white shirt with the sleeves rolled up over his well-muscled brown forearms. Since the demon kept glancing at his arms, Teri assumed the elf had calculated his look as specifically as the demon had hers. His bow and quiver leaned against the wall next to his chair, the quiver filled with blond-feathered arrows. They didn't have any drinks on the table. Or food. Just the chessboard. Since Teri didn't play chess, she had no idea how the game was going, but since the demon looked smug and the elf looked annoyed, she'd be willing to place money on the demon.

Behind them, in the far corner of the room, a group of dwarves sat around a much larger round table, shouting over one another to be heard, their pickaxes stacked in a pile in the corner. Their table was wet from all the spilled beer—such a waste!—and their bushy beards were peppered with the crumbs from their lunch. As she watched one pushed his chair back suddenly, the scrapping sound harsh over the wooden floor, and shouted something that sounded like a curse in that guttural dwarven language she'd never been able to master. The dwarf pointed a short stubby finger at another dwarf even as some of his companions rose to settle him back into his seat. There was much grumbling and a few more shouts before they settled back down and continued their animated conversation. All without throwing a punch or picking up a weapon. That was an impressive show of restraint.

Teri turned toward the bar on her left, the short curving counter scuffed and marked with oily streaks, showing its age in the well-worn black wood. Behind the bar, the pub proprietor wiped down the counter as he watched the dwarves closely, his eyes narrowed.

She strolled to the bar and set her backpack on the counter. "Hey, Jim," she greeted.

"Teri!" The man turned toward her, his shaggy blue hair and weather-worn pale face a sight for sore eyes. "Been ages. Good to see you back."

"Thanks. Can I get a stout? The good stuff."

"You got it." He held a thick ceramic jug under the tap at an angle and slowly pulled her drink, leaving a satisfying layer of thick creamy foam on top of the black beer.

Teri sighed in happiness again as Jim set the jug on the counter with a slight thump. "Finally," she murmured, taking a deep sip. The stout was thick and full of hops flavors with an undertone of caramel. Delicious. She had no idea why the people in the US thought what they drank was beer when it tasted like watered down piss. This was what beer was supposed to taste like. One of the others had claimed the beer in Ireland and Germany was better. But her mission had kept her in the US. She hadn't been able to get that far just for a beer. At least not this trip.

Shame, though.

"You hungry?" Jim asked, back to wiping down the already-immaculate countertop.

"Love a meat pastie. Better make that two." Her stomach grumbled. When was her last meal? Hours ago. Sometime that morning? It had been a drive-through and not even a little appetizing, though it had fueled her long enough to get here.

To get home.

"Coming right up," Jim said, and shouted back into the open door to the right of the bar counter. "Two pies, Maeve."

A higher voice shouted back out. "Two pies, coming up!"

"So how'd it go?" Jim asked her. "Get everything?" His gaze jumped to her backpack, but that was the only twitch. Otherwise, he kept his attention on her face, the pupils in his green cat's eyes long and narrow despite the dim lighting inside the pub.

"Got everything," she said with a nod. "Took bloody long enough." She gulped down another swallow of yummy stout. The sweat on her back had dried, leaving her almost chilled in the cool pub. But after the dry desert heat, the chill felt nice, the cool darkness soothing for her nerves.

"Been a while since you found us. I was starting to worry."

"Anjour around?"

"He'll be in later. You have time to eat."

She took her backpack and beer to the nearest free table, brushing a few crumbs off the wood onto the straw beneath before settling down, her backpack at her feet, her foot on the strap to keep it from "walking" off. There didn't seem to be any pixies hanging around up by the rafters, but you could never tell with those little thieves. And she couldn't afford to lose her backpack now. Not after all these months. Not after how hard she'd had to work to get everything.

Maeve swanned out of the kitchen with the two meat pies

on a little aluminum tray. "Teri! Good to have you back, love. You look good. World outside treated you okay?"

"Hey, Maeve." She grinned up at the woman—and up.

Maeve was easily seven foot tall, her black hair hanging around her thick shoulders in long braids and twists, all of it decorated in little silver clips and cylindrical, jewel-colored beads. Her sharp features were arranged in a way that brought to mind handsome and distinguished. No soft beauty for the elf matron. Nope, she was all powerful build and impressive countenance. Her pale white skin was damp and flushed from the kitchen, but she smiled wide as she set the delicious smelling meat pies in front of Teri.

"If those aren't enough, you just let me know, love," Maeve said. "I'll whip you up some more. Imagine you haven't had a good pastie since you left."

"Nothing as good as your food," Teri confirmed as she breathed in the thick, meaty gravy scent. The parchment paper wrapped around the hand pies showed dark spots from the flavorful grease still clinging to the fried crust—a perfect flaky shade of butter tan—and there were hints of the brown gravy leaking out of a small split in the pies seam. Teri's stomach growled again

"Give them a few seconds to cool," Maeve said. "Just out of the fryer."

Maeve waved to the dwarves when they shouted a greeting to her, then headed back to the kitchen through the open door. She had to duck to avoid knocking her head on the door frame.

Teri tucked into her pies, groaning when the rich, thick brown gravy hit her tongue. The pastry was as flaky and buttery as it looked. The meat, carrots, peas, and potatoes inside were cooked perfectly. And all that lovely gravy…

She'd really really missed Maeve's meat pasties.

She finished off her pies and beer quietly and quickly, listening to the pub noise, the occasional shout from the dwarves, the elf cursing when the demon got him in check. No one else came through the door until she had moved on to her second flagon of beer and was leaning back in her seat, prepared to wait out Anjour.

When he stepped through the pub's front door, a moment later, he brought a cold wash of rainy air on an oak and maple-scented wind.

And a sense of anticipation and worry that had Teri, very gently, setting down her beer.

*A*njour was old. Teri wasn't entirely sure how old. But he'd been around for longer than her life and the life of her mother before her. He didn't look particularly old. He didn't look young either. In fact, he was in many ways a very ordinary looking person.

For a watchman.

Average height—a little taller than her, significantly shorter than Maeve—brown hair threaded with gray, just brushing his shoulders, hazel eyes, a face full of soft angles, faint creases feathering out from his eyes, a short beard and mustache with more gray than brown in it, white skin under the beard that flushed easily with exertion. He wore tanned, beaten leather trousers and a leather duster that brushed the ground. His wide brimmed hat shadowed his forehead, but he'd pushed it back enough so she could look him in the eyes.

All in all, he was pretty human-looking, as unremarkable and non-descript as he could possibly be in his world.

A very deliberate ploy.

He'd surprised her by arriving earlier than she'd expected. It had taken her so long to return, so long to find the doorway again, she'd have thought he'd make her wait here through dinner. Now that the time had finally come, she found her stomach tightening, just a little, with worry. She knew she'd done a good job, accomplished exactly what she'd intended. Still, when dealing with Anjour, it was always best not to take anything for granted.

"Teri," he greeted, his voice high and pitched toward soft. "You've finally returned." He didn't look around the pub, but she noticed the background hum of noise and conversation had stilled.

She picked her beer up again and lifted her flagon to him in a small salute. "I told you I'd be here."

"Took you a while."

"You knew it would. You didn't exactly give me an easy quest." She motioned to the seat opposite her. "Sit. We have things to discuss."

"Yes."

He settled in the wooden chair keeping his gaze on hers, his mouth a straight line. She couldn't read his expression, couldn't guess what he was thinking, but then she'd never been able to read him.

"You had trouble?" he asked.

"Not with the collection."

He stared at her, his expression never changing.

She shrugged and rolled her eyes. "Okay, maybe a little trouble with the collection. The whole thing took longer than I thought it would. Finding humans who reach adulthood without any cynicism is harder than it sounds."

She wouldn't admit this out loud to Anjour, but it had been almost impossible. The human world leaned toward cynicism. She couldn't blame them. She was a bit of a cynic herself. It came with growing up and learning that other people could be hypocrites. Hard to avoid cynicism when hypocrisy was so rife.

"You got what you were sent for?"

She huffed out a breath. "Yes. Yes. I got all of it."

"And you found the doorway back."

Eventually. She kept that comment to herself, too. He didn't need to know that had taken her as long as it had.

The fact that it had taken her time, and effort, to find the door home was part of the quest anyway.

"I'll need to see," he said.

"I would have expected nothing less." She picked up her backpack and set it in her lap. The little bottles inside clinked gently together. Without any other conversation happening inside the pub, the sound of those bottles was loud. And obvious.

She opened the pack and pulled out the three glass jars one at a time, setting them gently on the table in a row. They were broad and thick, made of clear glass, but the substance inside was dark dark ebony, so dark it made the jars opaque. Their lids were all silver—real silver, pure silver—and covered in the sharp lines of runes that glowed faintly blue in the dim pub lighting. Other than the runes, the lids were plane, unadorned. Specific for their purpose of holding in this particular substance.

Anjour smiled at the jars, lifting one to inspect. "Perfect," he murmured. "You've done…an impressive job, finding all three."

"And it wasn't easy," she said. "If I'd known, I'd have charged you more."

His smile widened before dropping away as he inspected the second jar.

She knew all three were in perfect condition and all three contained exactly what he'd hired her to retrieve.

The tears of a truly sincere human. And adult. With no ounce of cynicism in their hearts.

An almost impossible quest. Anjour had paid her a pretty penny for the job. The rest of what he owed, to be paid in full on delivery, would set her up for the rest of the year. She could go home and rest. Spend time with her family. Which, after months of hunting through the human world for a way home, sounded like bliss.

A kind of peace she'd started to despair of ever having.

Because while taking a job from Anjour came with huge rewards, failure in these quests came with devastating consequences.

She suppressed her shiver. No need to think on that now. She'd made it back. She hadn't failed.

His smile had turned to a frown by the time he reached the last jar. This one… She remembered this person well. Gloria. Sweet. Strong. Sincere.

So very very angry.

The tears in that jar came from her anger. She hadn't been sad when she'd cried. She'd been in a rage. Over someone else's hypocrisy. Someone else's cynicism. Gloria had been magnificent in her rage. And she'd done something that even Teri's much more jaded heart wouldn't have expected. She succeeded in a lawsuit that brought about justice for a small hospital whose cancer patients had been harmed by the company she'd sued. She'd gotten justice in a system stacked against her.

That moment had been something to see. And the reasons Teri had dallied in the human world for so long before attempting to find the door to the pub. Just to see the ending of that case. Justice was a rare thing, often slipping under the weight of laws and precedents. And money. And corruption. Even without the last two though, justice wasn't always served in the human world. Not *real* justice. Mostly there were compromises made and things were arranged so neither side was completely happy, but some restoration of balance took place.

And Teri supposed that most of the time, that was the best that could be hoped for, the best possible outcome. But sometimes… Sometimes it was satisfying to see *real* justice done.

Gloria had managed that. In all her belief and righteous anger, she'd managed real justice without ever giving in to despair and cynicism. Her jar, the jar with her tears, was a prize.

"I should charge you more for that one," Teri said.

The already quiet room, if possible, got quieter. Not even the scrape of a chair over the wooden floor. Not even the sounds of breath.

Anjour glanced up from the bottle, his gaze holding hers for a long moment. She didn't blink. She knew what she'd gotten him there.

After a moment, his expression softened and he smiled. Around her, there were several gasps of indrawn breath, as if everyone had been holding theirs.

"There's a reason I hired you for this quest," Anjour said. "Where did you find this?"

"You paid for the jars, not the stories."

Those… Those she'd keep to herself. The people whose tears she'd collected, they deserved that much, a preservation of their privacy. Anjour didn't need the stories. He just needed the tears of those three very specific people.

He held her gaze a moment longer before shrugging. "Fair," he said. "And you're right. I've underpaid you." He lifted the final glass jar with Gloria's tears.

"You have. But a bargain set is a bargain made."

His lips twitched. "That's the other reason I hired you. Another bounty hunter would have tried to charge me more for this one."

"I'll just take what you owe me." If she played fairly with him, he'd hire her again. She could do worse than a steady stream of jobs for Anjour. They were never easy jobs. The consequences of failure, the risks in the jobs themselves… No, never easy.

But worth it. To her way of thinking.

Especially if it meant she could spend the rest of the year with her family without having to leave for yet another hunt.

He pulled a small bag from inside his duster and slid it across the table to her. She snatched it up, hefted it once to ensure the weight was appropriate, and then dropped it into her backpack, still on her lap.

"May I ask a question?" she said.

He motioned her to proceed with a single twirl of his hand.

"What does a watchman need with those?" She nodded to the jars.

Knowing was insignificant to her job. She was hired to collect difficult things, things that couldn't be found easily. What those things were, and what their ultimate purpose was, had very little to do with her. She tried to ensure what she found didn't harm others, no working for unscrupulous employers looking to destroy the worlds or anything. She only worked with clients she could trust.

Anjour, for all his ruthlessness if a hunter failed, was honest in his dealings. Everyone in this pub could vouch for that. She knew the dwarves had done work for him. And the demon. She wasn't so sure if the elf had. But at least one of the trolls had. All of them assured he was a fair client, and his aims weren't the sort of thing that might destroy others. He was a watchman after all. They watched. They ensured balance in this realm.

But why would a watchman need the tears of humans without any cynicism in their hearts?

She was a little worried about the level of cynicism in her own world if a watcher needed three jars of those tears.

Anjour glanced down at the jars, then up at her, his expression softened as he considered her, though his eyes were narrowed.

Another very obvious silence descended around the pub as the others waited, too.

CHAPTER 4

*A*fter a few more moments of utter silence, Anjour straightened and dropped his gaze. "I think that's a question…best left unanswered."

Hmm. Which meant what Teri had feared was likely the problem. There wasn't enough sincerity in their own world.

Balance had to be held.

"Fair," she said, her own eyes narrowing as she studied him. "I suppose I'm glad the watchers are…aware of all the issues," she said but also asked.

"They are very good at their jobs." He tilted one of the jars toward her. "Like you."

She grinned. "I am."

"Which is why you got this job." Anjour produced a small leather satchel from inside his duster and carefully placed the glass jars inside.

"Does that mean we can work together again?" she asked. Always good to establish with a client.

"I think we can. When I have another job for you, I can find you here?"

"You can find me here." In a few months. After she'd spent her well-earned down time with her family.

He stood and dropped the long strap of the satchel over his head and across his chest so the bag, and the bottles inside, settled at his hip. "Until then." He touched the brim of his hat. Glanced around the room.

From the corner of her eyes, she noticed several sudden movements, heads turned back toward their own tables or companions. Suddenly trying to appear like they hadn't been hanging on every word of her conversation with Anjour.

She huffed out a quiet chuckle.

Anjour's brow quirked, his only reaction. Then he swung back out the pub door, letting in another blast of rain-scented oaks and maple.

She pulled in a deep breath. Time to go home.

She emptied her flagon, letting the perfect stout slide down her throat in cool deliciousness. Then dropped a gold coin on the table. The familiar pawing lion on one side of the coin landing up. A good sign. The spiked branches on the other side of the coin boded more ominous tidings. Not that she believed that the random position of a coin meant anything. Not in real life. She'd let go a lot of her superstitions when she'd gone to work as a hunter. The world was a weird place. And random. But almost never was that randomness the result of a coin toss.

"On your way, Teri?" Jim asked from his spot behind the bar, still rubbing down the counter as if he hadn't just been watching her exchange with Anjour intently.

"Time to get home, Jim," she said, rising and shifting her backpack to hang over one shoulder.

"See you next time, then," he said.

Maeve poked her head out of the kitchen. "Have a good few months, Teri. Come see us again when you're ready."

"Thanks, Maeve." She motioned to the empty, neatly folded, grease-darkened parchment paper still on the table. "And thanks for the superb lunch."

Maeve waved that away as she ducked back into the kitchen.

One of the trolls grunted and raised his flagon to her as she headed out. She gave him a nod in return. Greetings among peers who avoided getting to know each other too well. A balance there, too. Know who the others were, know who she could trust and not trust, know who's word she could take on a client… But never too close. Never too much personal information.

You never knew when a hunter would fail and not return. Better never to get too close. Just in case.

She stepped out into the late afternoon sunshine, this light filtered through tall, thick trees dappling the rich brown earth and ferns under the canopy. The rain had stopped. Water dripped from the thick leaves overhead, a misting she didn't mind after the deserts she'd been driving through the last few weeks.

From the depths of an animal trail winding through the trees came a familiar shout.

"Mommy, mommy, mommy!"

She dropped to a squat and opened her arms wide as her seven-year-old son came bursting through the underbrush and launched into her arms. This was the best part of getting home. The part she waited for.

The part that balanced all her own cynicism.

"Hello, my love." She hugged Pippen tight. "Miss me, eh?"

"Always. You were gone longer this time."

Time worked differently in her world, so to Pippen she'd only been gone a month, maybe five weeks. Not the months and months she'd experienced, thankfully. Still for a seven-year-old that was a long time.

"It was a hard job." She leaned back and ran her hands over his cheeks, cupping his beloved face. "Your hair is longer. And you're taller! How did that happen?"

"Daddy made sure I ate well," he said with a definitive nod she knew meant Daddy had told him to say that.

She pressed her lips together to keep from grinning. "Shall we go home and tell Daddy what a good job he did, making sure you ate enough to grow another inch?"

Pippen grabbed her hand as she stood and tugged her toward the trees, leading her back down the narrow trail, toward home.

And her well-earned rest.

DESTINY THROUGH THE CATS EYES

CHAPTER 1

*E*rica Randal walked into her Aunt Jilly's small house hoping for the sound of her aunt's voice but expecting the ammonia stench of unchanged cat litter boxes and hot muggy air.

She got neither of those things.

"Aunt Jilly?" she called as she let herself in with her key.

Her aunt had given her that key three years ago, right before she'd moved to Chicago for her dream starting job as an assistant professor of social history at the university. The key was a promise that she'd always have a place to return to if she needed it. A promise that had made the move to Chicago from Upstate New York a lot easier.

But she wasn't here for her own needs right now.

She still couldn't believe it had taken her mother a week to tell her Jilly was missing!

On the flight here, Erica had just about convinced herself that her mother had something wrong. That it was a misunderstanding. That Jilly had just gone on a cruise and hadn't told her sister. That Jilly was mad at her sister for some reason and not taking her calls.

But Erica's mother had a key to Jilly's place too. She was convinced her sister was missing.

Since Jilly was as close to Erica as a sister, more so since Erica didn't have any siblings, Erica had taken the first flight she could get from Chicago to Buffalo. She'd come right here from the airport, willing Jilly to be here and this to be a mistake of some kind.

The air inside Jilly's small, one-story house was a little warm, like she hadn't bothered with the air conditioner yet even though it was the middle of the day and the temperature was climbing. It had been cooler overnight. September, rolling into October, tended toward cooler nights but some pretty hot days still. And this was one of those weeks. A good time to save money by shutting the air conditioning off as often as possible.

But since Jilly had a clowder of cats in her care, she didn't ever let the house get too hot. She kept it at a cat friendly temperature all year round, even if that meant driving up her electricity bill in the summer to keep the place nice and cool for her fury family. The fact that the air conditioner wasn't on yet, but the house didn't feel stifling hot, like it had been off for days, was encouraging.

The fact that no cats came to greet her, or at the very least inspect her, was less encouraging.

Nothing to panic about, though. Jilly's seven cats tended to keep to themselves and didn't deign to acknowledge visitors unless they were in a mood. None of them were particularly skittish around guests, except maybe Galahad. Galahad swanned out of the room every time she entered his space. She hadn't been able to befriend him at all. Jilly had claimed it was because he was more standoffish after losing his mother as a kitten.

But the rest of the cats… They tolerated people in their

space just fine. Sometimes they even greeted her like she belonged here—although that hadn't happened since she'd left for Chicago.

As she made her way through the familiar house, though, the fact that there were no cats coming out to greet her felt… off. Wrong.

She started her search in the living room with its oversized couch covered in blankets against the cat hair and a large flatscreen fixed to the wall over an unused fireplace. Nothing. She called her aunt's name as she checked the kitchen. Dishes in the dishwasher, but they were clean. The sink empty. There was food in the refrigerator, but not much —a gallon of milk approaching its expiration date and a pile of fresh cat food on the top shelf. Some apples in the fruit and veg drawer that still looked okay, but maybe getting close to not being edible anymore. She wasn't a big fruit person so all apples looked mildly inedible to her. There were some condiments in the fridge door, a frozen loaf of bread and some frozen meals in the freezer. But that was about it. Not a lot. Definitely not the full fridge Jilly usually kept.

Erica also took that as a good sign. That her aunt had planned to go away and wasn't missing.

The cats' food and water bowls were lined up neatly on a matt at one side of the small, eat-in kitchen, near the breakfast nook that looked out onto the backyard. There wasn't anything in the bowls. No water. No leftover food.

Was that a good sign or a bad sign?

When Jilly planned a trip, she usually got someone to come in and look after the cats. There were too many of them to take them to a cat hotel—or so Jilly told her. Erica didn't know the first thing about cat hotels—so Jilly hired a friend to come over and check on the cats twice a day if she went out of town. The first thing Erica had done after her mother's call was to call Jilly's usual cat sitter. Bethany hadn't been hired to cat sit. In fact, she said she hadn't spoken to Jilly in a few weeks.

Could Jilly have taken the cats to an outside place? Maybe she'd found somewhere that would keep all seven cats together?

Erica glanced briefly out to the backyard. No cats. No Aunt Jilly. Just a lot of wildly growing grass and flowers and weeds that Jilly said were good for the environment. Her annoying next door neighbor had other ideas, but Jilly just ignored the notes about needing to cut her grass. It was her backyard. The neighbors could, in Jilly's words, "Shove off."

There was a reason Erica loved her aunt so much.

She made a quick pass through the small laundry room off the kitchen, poked her head into the garage, also just off the kitchen. Jilly's Prius was still there, but that wasn't too suspicious. Jilly took taxis to the airport. If she'd gone on a trip, she would have left her car locked up in the garage.

Erica went deeper into the little house and checked in Jilly's office-crafting room. A combination of desk and computer on one side, a wall of supplies for a bunch of arts and crafts Erica had never gotten the hang of on the opposite wall. The computer was off. The supplies in the white shelves were all neatly tucked into their drawers and cabinets. Nothing was out on the small crafting table in front of the supply shelves.

Still no cats.

Finally, Erica turned toward the door to Jilly's bedroom. For all the time she spent in this house, she never went into Jilly's bedroom. The door was always closed. And it hadn't really occurred to Erica that she hadn't been in or even seeing the interior of Jilly's room in years. There was a small cat door set into the bedroom door, which Erica considered a bit eccentric. But the bedroom was where the cats retreated if they wanted to get away from visitors, so the cat door did make a strange kind of sense if Jilly also wanted to keep the door closed.

Erica stood in the hallway for a long moment. "Aunt Jilly?" she called.

She pressed an ear to the thin wood. No sound.

She really really didn't want to invade her aunt's privacy. But with no sign of the cats, and no sign of Jilly, and her mother filing a police report for her missing sister…

Erica turned the door knob, the smooth, cool brass giving easily. No lock. She pushed the door open and stood in the doorway blinking in the dimness, taking the place in.

Still no cats. And no overwhelming stench of cat boxes. Jilly was strict about the care and cleaning of the boxes so the house didn't stink. In fact, while the place did always smell like cats, and the cat hair built on the couch and carpets despite daily vacuuming, the house never smelled bad. Never that ammonia-heavy cat urine stench that could choke a person not inured to it.

If Jilly were missing, and the cats were still here, the place would stink by now. There'd be no getting around it. The entire house should have been overwhelmed by the stench of cat urine. And there would likely be a whole lot more yowling and hissing going on.

But there was no cat stink. And no cats.

Just a giant cat tree that took up one whole corner of the room. In fact, the floor-to-ceiling cat tree dominated the room. It was the largest thing in the space, even larger than her aunt's queen-sized bed. She'd never seen a cat tree that large.

It had several bases and branches rising to flat, circular platforms and enclosed boxes with small holes for the cats to slip in and out of. The whole thing was covered in a tan-colored carpet material, a rougher carpet wrapping around the columns, a softer, fluffier carpet cushioning the circular platforms and outside of the boxes. The central column was as thick as a real tree, almost as wide as her own shoulders. And as she looked at the tree from the doorway, she thought it actually looked more like a real tree than an artificial bit of furniture for cats to climb and claw without doing damage. She could see the tufts of black, white, and tan cat hair covering the tree even from a distance. And the smell in the room was definitely stronger cat.

But not litter box stench.

The boxes themselves were lined up at the opposite wall from the tree, near the open bathroom door. They looked clean and mostly unused. A very faint smell of the litter, and maybe a hint of bleach from the cleaner Jilly used on the boxes reached her. But no ammonia stink.

The rest of the room also looked neat and unused.

The bed was made, covered with a simple floral comforter and a small pile of pillows against the wooden headboard. The closet door was closed. The dresser was neat with the drawers closed and only a few items scattered across the top—a brush, a lipstick, a box full of loose change and various pocket paraphernalia, a small tissue packet. The bathroom also looked neat and unused. The glass door on the bath-shower was pulled closed but no towels hung on the rod. The towel on the rod behind the sink was dry and neatly folded. There were two toothbrushes in a cup beside the sink, and she wondered at the second brush since Jilly lived alone. But otherwise, there was nothing strange in the bathroom.

Everything looked the way it might if Jilly had gone traveling and wanted everything neat and clean for her return.

Except for the fact that there were no cats.

Erica put her hands on her hips and stared at the cat tree. Where were the cats? Jilly was adamant that they all stay together, and that no cat hotels could accommodate so many cats at once and still keep them together. Erica's mother was allergic to cat hair so she wasn't able to cat sit, but the usual sitter said she wasn't busy and would have been able to sit for Jilly if she'd asked.

Jilly was not here. But the house looked like she'd left on purpose. Like she'd planned a trip. Everything looked normal and innocuous and innocent.

Except for the missing cats.

Still staring at the cat tree, Erica pulled her cellphone from the back pocket of her jeans. She'd call her mother again, see what she'd learned. As she swiped the phone on, something at the cat tree moved. She'd caught the movement from the corner of her eye. But when she looked up, everything seemed unchanged. Erica frowned, looked down at her phone again.

More movement in her peripheral vision.

This time when she looked up, she spotted the sleek black fur of a long tail slipping through the cat tree, to a platform not in plain view.

The cats!

Erica hurried closer to the tree. There were two cats with black tails. Galahad—who'd avoid her—and his sire Memnon—her aunt had a habit of grandiose names for the cats. If it was Memnon, the other cats wouldn't be far behind. He was the definitive leader of the clowder. If cats could have a leader. She wasn't actually sure. But in her aunt's little group, Memnon was the one the other cats deferred to.

"Mem? That you?" she called, keeping her voice a little higher and softer than usual, hoping to lull the others out as well. "We thought you were missing. I was so worried."

The cat didn't reappear from behind the tree. She shifted to one side, trying to get a better view. And then another movement, from the thick central column of the tree caught her attention.

To Erica's relief and utter confusion, her Aunt Jilly stepped out of the cat tree.

She was dressed in brown leather pants and a loose cream shirt with a belt wrapped around her waist. A belt that had a *sword* in scabbard at her hip. Her gray-blond hair was pulled back in a tight braid. And she had a diadem on her forehead, with a central jewel that looked like a golden cat's eye.

Jilly looked up and spotted her before Erica had fully processed what she was looking at. This was definitely her aunt, but… Very much not the aunt she knew.

"Erica!" Aunt Jilly said, her normally soft voice louder and more commanding. "It's about time you got here. Hurry. We don't have time to waste. The realms need you."

CHAPTER 2

For several moments, Erica just blinked at her aunt, her mouth open. "Realms?"

Of all the questions she had, that seemed the easiest to get out. It only required one word and that was about all her brain seemed capable of at that moment.

Her aunt, wearing a getup right out of a Renaissance Faire, had just stepped *out* of the cat tree's central column. Like it was hollow. Like it was a door.

That…couldn't have just happened.

And though she hadn't seen them before, now all seven cats surrounded her aunt, most on higher platforms on the tree, but two of them on the ground at her aunt's booted feet. Memnon and Galahad, their black tails wrapped around their legs as they sat tall next to Jilly.

Erica opened her mouth to ask another question but the words weren't there. She didn't even know where to start.

"No time to explain here," Jilly said. "We have to go. You took a long time getting here."

She crossed to Erica and put her hands on her shoulders, forcing Erica to look her in the eyes. Jilly was about two inches taller than Erica's five-foot ten-inch height, but in that moment, the difference felt significant, forcing Erica to look up at her aunt in a way she hadn't done since she was a kid.

"I don't understand," Erica managed. "Mom thought you were missing. She's filed a police report."

Jilly's mouth tightened into a straight line. She shook her head. "Damn it. I didn't need that complication. Valerie really needs to mind her own business."

"She was worried about you!"

"There wasn't any need. What took you so long to get here?"

"Mom didn't tell me you were missing until yesterday. I got here as soon as possible."

"You…" Jilly frowned and glanced down at Memnon and Galahad. "You didn't get my message a week ago? I left a voicemail."

Erica still had her phone in her hand. She opened her voicemail app, double checked for a message from her aunt, and then showed her the screen. "No message."

"Well…" Jilly huffed out an annoyed breath, dropping her hands to her hips. "I can't believe everything nearly fell apart because a *voicemail* didn't get through." She rolled her eyes. "Anyway, you're here now. We don't have a lot of time. Let's go." She started tugging Erica back toward the cat tree.

"Wait. Go? Go where? What's happening? Jilly, stop. You need to tell me what's going on."

"Explanations on the other side. They'll make more sense there anyway. Come on." Jilly pulled her closer to the cat tree. "This will be a little disorienting at first. Don't worry if you have to throw up. The nausea will go away."

"Wait. Wha—"

She didn't have time to get the questions out before Jilly

stepped into the column of the giant cat tree, pulling Erica with her.

A moment of darkness. Some flickering, shadowed movement at the edge of her vision. And then she was out into bright sunshine, surrounded by a forest with trees that had trunks the size of small cars.

Erica blinked in the sunlight. Pine and cedar scented the air. The sky was blue and clear. A soft, chilly breeze moved through her hair, ruffling the baby hairs on her brow where they'd escaped her bun. At the edge of her hearing, she caught the booming thunder of a large waterfall. High up in the trees, birds unlike anything she'd seen before flittered and called to each other. They were all bright, neon-colored feathers and long, thick beaks. One landed on a lower tree branch long enough for her to realize the birds were huge. Larger than condors. With a wingspan when it lifted up that briefly blocking her view of the sky. That bird had to be as big as her.

A butterfly the size of her head flapped past, startling her, the spots on its wings looking like opening and closing cat's eyes. Erica watched it flutter toward a patch of red and purple flowers that vaguely resembled cornflowers but were easily the size of Jilly's cats. Everything here was *huge*.

Jilly stood in the middle of that giant forest surrounded by her seven cats, her Ren Faire costume somehow managing to fit into the setting. She looked larger than life herself. Somehow taller and more imposing. Like she belonged here. Like she was a part of this oversized world.

The golden cat's eye gem in her diadem glowed brightly, lit from within like a mini-star.

They weren't in Buffalo anymore.

Erica pressed a hand to her stomach, turned away from

Jilly, and abruptly sat on a large tree root coming out from the base of the nearest giant spruce tree.

"The nausea will ease," Jilly said again. "Don't worry. The first time through the portal is always a little disorienting. I had intended to do this in a less urgent moment, but… Well, things have changed. Are you better? Ready to go?"

"Portal? What? Go? No. Aunt Jilly." Erica gestured at their surroundings. "What's going on? Where are we? This definitely isn't New York."

In fact, the giant trees reminded her more of the giant redwoods in San Francisco. And the animals seemed more like something you might find in the Amazon. But the forest didn't *feel* like anything she might encounter traveling around the world. Certainly not like Illinois or New York. She'd never been to the Amazon, but it didn't *feel* like that either.

She wasn't sure what it was about the place. The air felt…charged. No, that wasn't quite right. Maybe static was a better way to describe it. Like her skin was sparking against something. Not painful. Not even really uncomfortable. Just…more energy in the air. And she felt more alive with all that energy touching off her skin, more…charged?

This was all just too strange.

She looked around for Jilly's cats. All seven had followed them through the cat tree and were standing in various places around Jilly. Memnon and Galahad at her feet. Jasper and Percival on the thick tree roots behind her. Morgaine crouched on a lower branch of a giant spruce. Odysseus on the ground a few feet in front of Jilly. And the last, Athena, farther to one side at the head of what looked to be a rough dirt path winding through the trees.

Jilly made a gesture toward the path. "We should move. I'll explain more as we walk."

"Where are we?" Erica said, rising to her feet, but wobbling a little on her unsteady knees.

Galahad made a jumping motion toward her, which was strange since he usually moved away from her, but when she steadied with a hand on a giant rough tree trunk, he stepped back to Jilly's side.

The hand she placed against the trunk connected with a small patch of sticky sap that left her hand smelling of spruce pine. Not a bad smell at all, but since she wasn't supposed to be surrounded by spruce trees right now, it wasn't a reassuring smell either. She rubbed her hands together in an attempt to get the sap off as she tried taking in more of her surroundings, hoping for sight of something familiar. It was just giant trees as far as she could see and the crystalline blue sky overhead.

"Where are we?" she murmured again.

"That's…a little difficult to say," Jilly said, then motioned again toward the path where Athena stood and started in that direction.

The moment she moved, so did all the cats, they fanned out in front and around her, Athena and Odysseus taking lead down the path, Memnon at Jilly's side, the others fanning out around Jilly.

Except for Galahad. Galahad waited, staring up at Erica. Erica frowned down at the cat. He was a large cat, long soft fur, mostly black with patches of white on his chest and back. His black tail twitched as he stared at her. He had his sire's eyes. Very blue. The kind of blue that really popped against his dark fur.

Something in his eyes she hadn't seen before made her blink. Not that she knew Galahad very well. He avoided her all the time. But…there was something more looking out at her from those cat's eyes now. Something she couldn't put her finger on.

She continued to frown down at Galahad. He continued to stare up at her.

With a huff of irritation and confusion, she hurried to catch up to Jilly. Galahad stayed at her side, walking as close to her as he'd ever gotten to her before.

Okay. That was really strange. As strange as anything else that was happening. And there were a *lot* of strange things happening.

"Aunt Jilly, why do you have a sword?" Erica asked because she couldn't get over her crafting, cat-lady aunt having a sword strapped to her hip as she stalked through a forest full of giant trees like she was some sort of…warrior woman or something. Even more unsettling was how *right* Jilly looked walking through the giant forest like a warrior woman.

"Necessary evil here, I'm afraid," Jilly said, patting the sword's rounded pommel.

"And, once again, where is here?"

"Yes. That. Well. See. Our family isn't precisely…what's written on the label."

"I… Huh?"

"Not everyone. Your mother and your Aunt Rita are perfectly normal. This sort of thing only happens to one person in each generation, and I was the lucky one in mine." She glanced over her shoulder. "You were the lucky one in yours."

She didn't feel like the "lucky" one right now. She just felt overwhelmingly confused.

"The thing is, we're…" Jilly sighed. "How to put this? Editors isn't right. Collectors? Not quite. Though there is an element of that. But… No. I suppose calling us guardians is as good a word as any."

"Guardians?" Erica shook her head.

"Not my favorite," Jilly said with a self-deprecating shrug, "but it is the one that's used most often. It's the one my aunt used. I suppose after all these years I should just learn to accept it."

Erica blinked at Jilly's back. "Guardians of what?"

"That'll be easier to explain when we get there. But just know, it's a very necessary role. Keeps this whole place from tipping into a war that would destroy everything."

"Huh?" She couldn't manage much else. Nothing Jilly was saying made the least bit of sense.

"Yes, I suppose without seeing the temple, it's impossible to understand the whole thing. Still. What I'm trying to tell you is that the time for you to take up your training as a guardian is a little late. We should have started this a few years ago. Balance needs to be maintained. But you moved away, and I wanted you to have a choice in what your life became so I neglected my own duty and now here we are."

"Not a single thing you've just said makes anything that's happening clearer."

"I know. I'm mucking this up. Don't worry. It'll make sense soon."

"Aunt Jilly, please. Stop. Just… Just tell me what's going on."

Jilly did stop. So abruptly Erica bumped into her back. Jilly turned and gripped her shoulders, steadying her but also holding her in place.

"My love, I'm afraid you have a terrible, wonderful destiny. And that destiny is to ensure the sacred texts are collected and protected so that neither the Wraith-sworn nor the Elder-sworn get to them. If either race acquires these texts, there will be a deadly war of such magnitude it will spill over into our realm and cause the destruction of all you've ever known."

Erica blinked up at Jilly again. That didn't sound good. Not even a little bit good.

"Preventing that is a sacred duty," Jilly continued. "One I'd hoped you could avoid, but… I was wrong. Just as my aunt was wrong before me. The duty can't be abandoned. We must continue. And that means, my lovely niece, the time has come for you to walk your path."

"I…I can't. I have a job. A life. Somewhere…else." She glanced around at the giant trees, the giant birds occasional fluttered through the branches overhead.

"You'll be able to keep up your life in our realm. In fact, that's an important part of all this. You'll just have this… other thing to do on occasion." Jilly shrugged. "It isn't so bad. Kind of a nice break from the day-to-day really."

Erica wanted to laugh. Not so bad? A break from the day-to-day? Jilly had gone absolutely mad. This was…

Impossible.

Right?

Jilly tugged her hand. "Let's get moving. Seeing the temple will help all this settle."

Erica stumbled forward after Jilly, glancing behind her in some sort of vain effort to find an exit. To return to reality. She was extremely grateful her aunt wasn't actually missing, but all this was too much. She had to be hallucinating. Which meant Jilly could still be missing.

She shook her head. None of it made sense and despite her senses telling her everything around her was real, she just couldn't believe it.

A sound overhead, a screech that ended in a sort of moaning sound made Erica stop in her tracks. Galahad, who had never touched her before or allowed her to touch him, bumped against her leg, repeatedly, as if trying to get her to move.

"Hurry," Jilly said, looking up at the sky. "We can't afford to get caught out here."

"Caught?" Erica rushed forward. "Caught by what?" That screeching-moan hadn't sounded like it belonged to something she wanted to meet face to face.

"The Wraith-sworn. They're circling. We need to reach the temple."

She glanced up, despite herself, but all she saw was the blue sky and the arching branches of giant spruce trees. Pine needles and cones littered their path, filling the air with a lovely fresh scent. But something about the changing lights and shadows had Erica's hackles rising, the fine hairs on her arms lifting as if a cold breeze had just brushed her skin. Yet there weren't any clouds moving by above to explain the changing light.

"What are Wraith-sworn?" she asked, her gaze on the sky.

"Nothing you want to face unprepared," Jilly said.

"Maybe not even face once you are prepared," a deeper voice said.

*E*rica blinked and stopped in her tracks, her heartbeat pounding. That deeper voice had come from right behind her. Shit. Panic gripped her and she started to jump forward, toward her aunt. Who had the sword.

But Jilly didn't even turn around. She kept marching forward down the narrow path, pushing aside ferns and occasionally glancing at the sky.

"Hurry," Jilly said. "Don't slow down."

Erica, her body starting to shake from the adrenaline rush of fear, glanced over her shoulder. A man she'd never seen before was there, following them, also glancing up at the sky. He was taller than Jilly by several inches, with thick black hair that brushed his shoulders and blue eyes that popped against his pale skin and dark, heavy eyebrows. His mouth was a hard line in a face that was exceedingly handsome. If he hadn't been scowling, maybe she'd have even called him stunning. He wore a similar getup to Jilly—brown leather pants, a loose-fitting white pullover shirt and a belt wrapped around his hips that held a sword.

She swallowed hard at the sight of that sword.

But he wasn't attacking anyone. He was marching right along behind them, glancing at the sky, and scanning the surrounding trees.

When he saw her looking at him, he motioned forward. "Don't slow down. You heard the guardian. Move."

She opened her mouth to say something, but she'd forgotten words again. There didn't seem to be any there. She was pretty sure she had questions. Lots and lots of questions. But the panic and fear and confusion had wiped away her ability to turn those questions into something coherent that she could communicate to other people.

She faced forward again, hurrying to catch up to her aunt and looking around for the cats. Memnon was still at Jilly's side, but the other six cats had disappeared.

Then, from the left, a woman stalked out from the woods and joined them on the path, just in front of Jilly. She had a sword at her hip too.

Erica opened her mouth to shout a warning, when another man stepped out of the trees on the right and also formed up in front of Jilly. Jilly didn't even pause at the appearance of the newcomers. And she didn't pull her sword.

The newcomers didn't do any attacking either.

Who the hell were these people?

"We'll explain when we're in the temple," the man behind her said.

He was close enough the sound of his voice made her jump and she had to press her lips together so she didn't squeak. Damn it.

Where the hell was this temple?

Three more people appeared from the trees, forming up around them like a phalanx, with her and Jilly in the center. Erica tried not to trip over her own feet, but it was difficult on the rough terrain, her tennis shoes built for city sidewalks not hikes in the woods, and all the shocks assaulting her system.

Who the hell were these people? Jilly didn't pause as they formed up around her. She didn't even glance at them. And the strangers didn't glance at her or Jilly either. Their attention all seemed to be on the surrounding forest and the sky overhead.

Another long moaning screech shattered the quiet, setting Erica's flight instinct into overdrive. She ducked her head a little for reasons she couldn't entirely explain and glanced up. Still nothing she could see, but the shifting shadows seemed to have increased. Like there were clouds rolling in. But she didn't see any clouds directly overhead. Only blue sky.

"They're closing in," the man behind her shouted forward.

"Almost there," Jilly shouted back.

As if that was a signal Erica didn't understand, everyone broke into a jog, not a full out run, but definitely moving faster, despite the uneven ground and narrow path.

The man behind her, already close enough she could feel the heat pumping off him, leaned closer and said, "Faster. Run if you can. We're almost there."

She wasn't sure her legs were steady enough for a full run, but since her flight instincts were ramped up, the thought of running also seemed like a very very good idea. She jumped forward into a jog that matched the pace of the others. She wasn't a runner, but she did go for long walks at home, and did cardio at the gym twice a week, so her fitness wasn't a complete disaster. Still, the jog left her panting, her heartbeat pounding hard.

Or maybe that was the fear.

Something briefly cut out the light overhead, a deep shadow that dropped the surroundings into darkness for a moment. The temperature, already mild, almost chilly, seemed to plummet in that moment too, turning icy in an instant. And in the next instant, warming again as the shadow lifted and sunlight once again filtered through the pine needles overhead.

Erica did trip this time, because the coordination necessary to jog and look up at the same time had apparently abandoned her. She stumbled and nearly went down, but a hand caught her elbow, keeping her upright. With remarkable ease.

Once she got her feet under her, she turned to the man behind who'd kept her from face-planting. "Thanks," she said.

He dropped his hold on her arm and grunted. "Keep going. We don't want to fall behind the others."

She hurried to catch up with Jilly but kept her gaze on the path so she didn't fall again.

Another shadow passed overhead. She resisted the urge to look.

And then the trees in front of their group opened up and there, in the middle of all the spruce and redcedars, stood a huge…

Pyramid.

A literal, pyramid.

Erica gaped at the sight. A pyramid. In the middle of the giant spruce tree forest. The two things just didn't go together in her brain. She associated pyramids with deserts or with thick tropical jungles. Not that she was an expert on pyramids or anything. Still. She just didn't have a reference point for a golden pyramid in the middle of pine country.

Made of tan sandstone bricks that gave the temple a golden glow in the sunlight, it was stacked in rough steps up to a flattened peak, each level easily her height which made the "steps" something she couldn't have climbed, even if she'd wanted to. At the center of the base was a large, rectangular break in the bricks, like a doorway, surrounded by smaller stones that seemed to have writing on them of some kind. The inside of the opening was too dark to tell if it led into an open tunnel or if there was a door beyond.

There were statues of sitting, stylized cats on either side of that entrance, recessed into the sandstone, but spanning the full height of the doorway. Which as they neared, she realized was even taller than she'd first thought. The base stones were all easily seven foot high, taller than Jilly by a good foot or more. The nearer they got, the larger the pyramid seemed.

She stopped to stare up at it, awed and confused and overwhelmed.

The man behind her set a hand to her back. "We don't have time to stop."

His voice was gentler than it had been up to that point, but still urgent.

His urgency got her moving again, until she'd caught up with the others at the entrance.

Now she could see the dark wooden door just inside the entrance, at the base of a shallow tunnel. Jilly was already in front of that door, doing…something. Erica couldn't really see her beyond a faint golden glow that seemed to surround her. The other people who'd joined them had all formed up around the entrance, their gazes scanning the forest and the sky.

Erica glanced up. The sky opened overhead now that they weren't under the tree canopy. All blue and cloudless and bright. Then something dark moved across that blueness. She couldn't make it out clearly. It was as insubstantial looking as a cloud, but a dark stormy raincloud. Ominous as it flew overhead, moving fast. Too fast. Faster than the gentle ground-level breeze warranted.

"What…?" she muttered.

"Wraith-sworn," the man who'd kept her moving said.

"I'm gonna need an explanation soon," she said, her gaze still on the sky.

"Soon," he said, his voice low, "when we're safely inside."

"*Will* we be safe inside?" she asked looking at him.

His mouth flattened into a harder line and he looked up at the sky. He didn't answer her question.

That wasn't even a little reassuring.

A sound like a *ca-chunk* and then a soft, sandalwood-scented breeze brushed her face. She looked down to see Jilly motioning her inside the pyramid.

"Hurry," Jilly said, as she came forward just enough to look up at the sky. She shook her head and waved everyone to move faster.

Erica didn't have to be told twice. The sensation of something overhead, something…stalking them, made her skin crawl and her nerves jump. She couldn't see what the Wraith-sworn were, exactly, but she could feel the menace in the air.

Or maybe it was just the jumpiness of the others. All she'd seen was a dark cloud moving too fast through the sky. But when she met her aunt's eyes as she passed her moving into the temple, she saw her own unease reflected there, and her aunt's jumpiness only made hers worse.

Jilly got everyone inside, she and Memnon the last to duck through the giant, wooden door.

The minute they were inside, the door closed, plunging the surroundings into darkness.

Erica almost panic. She almost screamed. After the bright

sunshine, the nerve-jangling sense of being followed, the strangers surrounding her and Jilly like guards, and the overall strangeness of this moment, being dropped into sudden, all-consuming darkness was more than Erica's nerves could take.

When a warm palm touched the small of her back, she jumped and only kept from screeching aloud by clenching her teeth tight together. She must not have succeeded, because a voice, low and close to her ear, said, "It's okay. Just me. You're fine. The lights will come up soon."

Just me was the man who'd been at her back the whole time. But him saying "it's just me" like that was supposed to be comforting was ridiculous. He was a stranger. She didn't know his name. She had no reason to be comforted by the fact that he was right next to her in the dark, his big hand against her lower back like it belonged there.

The weirdest thing, though, was that she did feel comforted by his presence. And his hand did feel like it belonged on her, warm and reassuring and strong in the middle of all this upheaval.

That was something she'd have to parse out later when she got home.

If she got home.

She waited in the dark, trying not to hyperventilate, until at last she realized she could see. Not much, but she could see a little through the gloom. Enough to see the shapes of the others looming large around her in a tight group.

The soft shuffling of feet a moment later. And then more light. She blinked as her surroundings slowly came into view.

And the very first thing she noticed was that the light was coming from Jilly's raised sword. Which now glowed a bright blue.

Erica hadn't seen the sword pulled from its scabbard

before this. Had it always glowed like that? The colored light made it impossible to inspect the weapon, but the blade seemed to have incandescently white lines running through the blue. It was as long as Erica's arm, thick, and came to a pointed tip that didn't look blunted. The fine edges didn't look blunted either. In fact, everything about the sword looked…sharp.

"Uhm?" she said, nodding to the sword and the light it created.

"I'll explain soon," Jilly promised.

"I've heard that a lot in the last twenty minutes, and I'm still as confused as I was when you stepped out of the cat tree."

"I know. I'm sorry. This really isn't how I intended on introducing you to all this." Jilly lifted the sword a little. "For the record, this is Alendrial, and you'll be inheriting her when you take over as guardian."

"Alendrial? The sword has a name? And is…female?"

"Yes. And yes. You'll understand when she's ready to be passed to you."

"Uh huh." Erica swallowed. "And when will that be?"

"Oh, not for a few years yet."

Jilly's smile was fast and so familiar it almost took Erica's breath away. Her aunt. Right there. And yet…the woman holding the glowing sword over her head was nothing like the Aunt Jilly Erica had always known.

"I still have some time left in these old bones," Jilly said with a chuckle.

"You're not old. Not even a little."

"Thank you," Jilly said. "But I'm…more aware now, shall we say, of my human aging. And that I've neglected a very specific duty for the last three years. That neglect almost bit us all in the ass."

Jilly had always been the cool aunt. The one who cursed and ignored her sisters' admonishments not to cuss in front of the kids. So Jilly using the word ass wasn't unusual. It just hit differently this time because she was dressed like a Ren Faire cosplayer and was holding a sword.

"Please don't make me wait for an explanation much longer," Erica said with a sigh. "This is overwhelming enough as it is."

"I'm so sorry, love," Jilly said, her flash of humor dying. "I will explain. Everything. But it's better if you see the sacred books first."

"Sacred books. Of course." She sighed. "Can those cloud-looking things get in here?"

"You saw a Wraith-sworn?" Jilly frowned at the man at Erica's back, then down at Memnon, before looking at Erica again. She touched the cat's eye jewel in the center of her diadem with her free hand, almost absently, like she didn't realize she was doing it.

"I wasn't supposed to?" Erica asked.

"It's not that… What did you see?"

"A dark storm cloud racing through the sky too fast for the actual air movement. I only know it's a Wraith-sword because he told me." She pointed to the man behind her. With a grunt, she faced him. "Probably introductions are in order too." She gestured at the others. "Lot of strangers here. And what happened to the other cats. Are they okay?"

She had no doubt Jilly's cats, like most cats, could hide well enough. But shouldn't Jilly be worried about where they were and the fact that they weren't safe inside the temple?

Even as this thought occurred to her, she realized how strange it was that none of the cats were here except for Memnon. And that Jilly wasn't looking for them. Or worried about them. And that instead there were people here.

The same number of people as there'd been cats.

She scowled up at the man behind her with the black hair and blue eyes. Eyes with the pupils narrowed now. Into slits. Like a cat's.

Cats standing guard outside the pyramid.

She narrowed her eyes at the man.

"If you tell me you're Galahad," she said to him, "I'm gonna know I've lost my mind."

The man's eyebrows popped up at Erica's declaration. "You… You know?"

Erica closed her eyes and shook her head. "Of course." She faced Jilly again. "All your cats are…" She gestured at the people.

Jilly smiled, proudly, as if Erica had just done something praise-worthy. "The fact that I didn't have to explain that, that you figured it out on your own, means I haven't made a mistake. You are the future guardian."

"Don't count on it. It's pretty obvious. And also, I'm pretty sure I'm crazy now, so…" She shrugged and huffed out a laugh that was more hysterical than amused. "So… All the cats are, what? The guardians of the guardian? And they can be people or cats. Like shapeshifters?"

"They can only be people here," Jilly said. "Except…" She glanced down at Memnon. Who was still very much a cat. "Well, most of them can only be people here. In our realm, their cat forms dominate. They can be either cat or human here. Most of them."

"Uh huh. Sure. Why not." When one realizes they've lost their minds, it becomes a lot easier to accept the ridiculous and nonsensical.

Jilly, still holding the glowing sword in one hand to light the dark surroundings, placed her other hand on Erica's shoulder. "It'll make sense soon," she said. "When you've had time to get used to it."

"Right." Because getting used to all this was definitely something she'd be able to do.

"How about I turn the lights on?" Jilly said. "Then we can talk." She glanced up at the ceiling, hidden in shadows, and despite herself, Erica looked up too. "We should have enough time."

Should have enough time?

That didn't bode well.

Jilly patted Erica's shoulder, then stepped to one side, still holding the sword high over her head. The blue light illuminated the space just inside the temple entrance in weird shadows and colored all the surrounding cat-guard-humans in blue, making them look almost alien.

What Erica could see of the interior of the temple was… not much. Stone. She thought. The floor was definitely stone. And there was a solid enough stone wall in front of her. They seemed to be standing in a smallish room. An antechamber maybe? The ceiling felt high overhead, and when she'd followed Jilly's gaze up, she hadn't been able to see anything, the sword's light not penetrating the deep darkness. So it felt high. But for all she knew, it was only a foot or two over her head. The sides of the small room were also hidden in shadows, so she couldn't tell if that darkness was tunnels branching off this area, or that the room was just a lot wider than it was deep.

There wasn't anything written on the wall in front of her that she could see. No embossed images. Just plain stone, light in color like the stones that had made up the outside of the pyramid. Probably. When they were blue-washed in the sword's glow, it was hard to tell their real color.

There wasn't anything on the floor. Just the smooth stone. No rugs or carpets or writing. No objects standing around.

She watched Jilly closely as she walked down a section of the back wall, running her hand over the stone. When she stopped, she pressed the wall a little, and for some reason Erica expected a door to open. Instead, Jilly raised her sword higher, and then plunged it into the spot on the wall.

The blade slid through the stone like butter.

Which would have been really impressive. If the next moment hadn't been even more awe-inspiring.

The surrounding stones flashed with a blinding wash of white light, the very walls lighting with an internal golden glow that lit the room up so suddenly, Erica winced.

Several moments of blinking passed before she could see again.

Once she could, the sight was…not at all what she'd been expecting.

They weren't in a small antechamber at all. The wall in front of them was just a sort of half wall in the middle of a huge, open space. The entire temple, all the way up to the peak, was open. There weren't corridors, or rooms that she could see. Just this giant single space with a small wall just inside the door that had given the illusion of sectioned areas.

And the giant, open, glowing space was filled with books.

Not just shelves of books, although there were those, but piles of books. Books on top of pedestal stands. Books in columns and towers of their own. Books stacked against walls. Books organized into mini-pyramids. Books on tables. Books in hanging baskets. Books…everywhere. All along the base of the pyramid, but also in shelves, and stacks going all the way up to the ceiling on balconies accessed by both rope ladders and wooden ladders.

Erica dropped her head back to stare up. The interior of the pyramid had progressively shrinking galleries. And while the walls of those galleries were angled inward, forming the pyramid shape, on each gallery were rows of freestanding shelves. Lined with books.

So. Many. Books.

Not like any library she'd ever seen in her life. Including some of the pictures of the most impressive libraries in the world.

Her historian's heart did a few happy leaps. The happiness was offset by a lot of confusion, though. "I'm not sure what to say about all this, but…wow. And maybe, huh?"

Beside her, Galahad's lips quirked in a quick-and-gone smile she almost missed.

"Aunt Jilly," she murmured. "What is all this?"

"A great deal of knowledge from a great many realms," Jilly said, quietly, almost as if they were in a library where they had to remain hushed. But there was also a lot of awe in her voice.

Erica could relate to the awe.

"This is what we protect," Jilly said. "This is the heart of so much knowledge. Some of it is too dangerous to land into the wrong hands."

"You haven't read all this?"

"Oh no. Some of it is in languages that would cook a human brain." Jilly laughed.

Erica didn't. Why was that funny? That wasn't funny.

"Don't worry, we keep those titles on the high shelves." Again another chuckle. "But there is an inventory list so we know what's here."

"That list must be miles long?" Erica said, her gaze still trained upward.

"Quite extensive at this stage, yes. And when we find another book that belongs here, we retrieve it."

"I thought you were a guardian of some kind. Not a librarian."

"I'm not the librarian," Jilly said. "My job is, primarily, to bring the books together and ensure they are safe. Memnon is the librarian."

"Huh?" Erica finally looked at her aunt. And took several steps back when she realized a stranger was standing next to Jilly.

But the black hair, the blue eyes, the general resemblance to the human Galahad… The biggest difference was this man was only as tall as Jilly, maybe even closer to Erica's height. And he had white streaks feathered in his black hair.

"Memnon?" she asked him.

He nodded. "It's good to finally meet you like this," the human who had just been a cat and was apparently also a librarian said.

"Uh huh," Erica said.

His grin was fast and stunning. Like a weapon all its own. He was as handsome as his son. Though he was obviously older, a few lines around his eyes, a few deeper dents bracketing his mouth, the two men had definitely fallen from the same tree.

Then she saw the way Memnon and her aunt looked at each other. It was a passing glance. But there was years of understanding in it. Years of coordination and unspoken conversation in that single look. And an intimacy that went beyond colleague.

Well. Good going, Aunt Jilly. Erica pulled in her lips so

she wouldn't grin. Instead, she took in her surroundings again. "This is…a lot."

"Would you like a tour?" Jilly asked.

"Maybe just the lower level. I'm pretty sure I want to avoid the brain-melting books."

"For now." Jilly turned and walked around the small half wall without explaining that ominous statement.

Erica scurried after her, circling the half wall, to see the temple's main floor without that last barrier. Yup. Lots of books.

Here she saw more clearly the shelves with scrolls capped in copper and tablets of stone stacked in neat piles, all interspersed with leather-bound hardbacks, and even some books that looked like paperbacks. There were rugs on the floor and some chairs scattered between the stacks of books, as well as a few thick cushions tossed randomly over the floor.

And to the right, what looked like another giant cat tree stood in one corner of the pyramid, up against the inward angle of the wall. This tree was carpeted in a brilliant deep cobalt.

Erica gestured at it. "Can you move through that one too?"

"That…gets you somewhere you're not ready to go yet," Jilly said.

Erica blinked at Jilly's back. She'd meant her question as a joke.

That would teach her to joke about cat trees being portals to weird worlds.

Jilly paused in the dead center of the pyramid and gestured to the stacks and piles and shelves. "These are the sacred texts. These are what we protect. What you were destined to protect."

"How? Why? And just from these Wraith-sworn and Elder-sworn whatever they are, or others?"

"The why is family legacy. Passed down for eons. There's a book here all about that."

"Of course there is."

Jilly's grin flashed again. "The how… Training. You'll start your training now. We've waited too long as it is."

"Training…what? With the sword?" Erica nodded to Alendrial, which Jilly had returned to the scabbard at her hip after pulling it from the false wall.

"Eventually. But also, as it turns out, you have some unique skills that are specific to the position of guardian. Those skills are what you'll start training first."

"What skills? I'm not a librarian."

"As I said, that's not your job. That's Memnon's for now. And will be Galahad's eventually."

Erica glanced back at Galahad. He didn't comment. Or look at her. Which for some reason struck her as telling. Though what his lack of eye contact was telling her, she couldn't say.

She faced Jilly again. "Then what *skills* do I have? I'm not a fighter. Never even taken a martial arts class."

"It's not that kind of skill I'm talking about either. As I said, we'll get to that part of your training later. First, you need to learn how to read."

"Uhm, I know how to read, Aunt Jilly."

She grinned, a quick flash of the humor Erica knew so well. "Ah, but you don't know how to read these books."

"How does me learning to read stop the Wraith-sworn from…, Well, whatever it is they were going to do before I got here? How is my being here important *now*?"

"Follow me. I'll explain."

"You keep saying that. I'm starting to not believe you."

Jilly gestured at the books. "This library, this storage unit, holds the knowledge of many realms and world. With it, the Wraith-sworn and the Elder-sworn would do terrible things. Have done terrible things in the past."

"War you said."

"War, yes. War that would spill into our realm. Wars that could destroy so much. But worse."

"What's worse than war?"

"Plague, famine, death…" Galahad said from behind her.

She startled a little at his voice. She hadn't realized he was following. And following so closely.

She glanced back at him. "Basically the four horsemen of the apocalypse, then?"

"Precisely," Jilly said, without irony. "And worse. Torture and slavery and all the other horrors you might imagine. All turned loose by either the Wraith-sworn or the Elder-sworn if they every gained access to the temple."

"And how do we know this?"

"They've done it before."

Jilly stopped at a table that held a single, simple wooden bookstand. And on the bookstand was a large, thick book bound in black leather and cmbossed with symbols on the cover that Erica couldn't read. There was a stylized cat on the spine, which looked remarkably similar to the cats guarding the entrance to the temple. The black leather looked worn but soft and subtle, not cracking or dry. And the closer Erica got to it, the stronger the scent of old leather and ink. A surprisingly comforting scent.

Jilly set her hand on the book. "This is the history of those times. They came and went before humans walked the Earth. This place existed eons before our species came to being and will exist long after we're gone. *If* we don't fail in our duty to protect it."

"Why *is* it our duty?"

"It's the duty of all the realms, and it just happens to be our turn."

Jilly said that so matter-of-factly Erica sighed. None of this was matter-of-fact. How could Jilly be so casual about it all? "So…how long are we humans in charge?"

"Just another couple of centuries before a new group takes over." Jilly blinked hard a few times. "And I very nearly ruined those last few centuries by stalling before introducing you to all this."

"Why us, then? Why our family?"

"That…that I don't know. It's something that's been passed down for generations back to my great-great-great multiple times over grandmother. But why *our* family…? It's not in the book. If anyone ever knew, they didn't record it. I only know that it's our responsibility and has been for many lifetimes. No one else is coming to help. All you see here? We're it."

"That doesn't sound good."

"You'd be surprised what we can do with so few, though."

For reasons Erica didn't fully understand, she glanced at Galahad.

"Now," Jilly said, drawing her attention back. "The reason the Wraith-sworn have gotten this close, the reason they're circling and attacking *now* is because, well, you're late. You're late to start training, to start reading. They can sense the thinning of the barrier, if you will, between one guardian and the next. And they're here to take advantage of that."

"So, all I have to do is start reading these books and all's well in—" She glanced around, frowning. "In wherever we are, I guess. Where are we?"

"The temple realm." Jilly raised her hand when Erica

opened her mouth to ask more questions. "That's the only name for it I have. There is no other name, not that I've heard of."

"Fine. You said I had a unique skill for this. What? Because I'm pretty sure reading isn't unique to me."

"No. But you're a historian."

"That's not particularly unique either."

While her general specialty—social history—was relatively new, with a focus on the day-to-day lives of ordinary people in the past, it still wasn't particularly unique. At least not unique to her. There were a dozen other faculty members in her general field just at her university. Not to mention the graduate students studying the various parts of social history.

"You see the world in a way that others don't," Jilly continued, "even in your study of history."

Erica supposed that was true enough. Her boss had often pointed out that she came to ideas and history in a way that the others in the department didn't. But she still didn't see how that qualified her to be the guardian of all the most sacred knowledge in multiple realms.

"And you can tease out the details you need to connect information in a way that others just…can't," Jilly said. "This place needs not just a librarian to organize the collection, not just guards to prevent break ins. This place needs someone who can…*understand* the knowledge here. Someone who can hold that knowledge together, see the ties between it all. The place *needs* someone to *know* it. And only you can do that."

"What about that brain-melting stuff?"

"You don't have to understand everything," Jilly said primly.

Erica might have chuckled if she weren't still so overwhelmed and confused.

Jilly motioned her around to stand next to her, in front of the black leather book. "Open the book."

"Am I going to pass out or something?"

"No, no. Don't be silly." Jilly met her gaze. "Do you trust me?"

"Of course." At least, she always had. From an early age, Jilly had been there for her, encouraging her when others thought her dreams were useless. She'd trusted Jilly to tell her the truth. And Jilly had never pulled her punches with her honesty. But her honesty had come with all the encouragement Erica needed.

Did she still trust Jilly?

There were some pretty big secrets Jilly had kept from her all these years. This place, the fact that her cats weren't ordinary cats…

Again, Erica found herself glancing at Galahad. He met her gaze, his somber but unflinching. The other cat-human-guards had all fanned out around the temple. Only Galahad and Memnon had stayed with her and Jilly.

Galahad might have walked away from her in his cat form, but now he seemed determined to stick close.

And for the life of her, she couldn't figure out why that was so comforting.

She met Jilly's gaze again. "Okay, I trust you. I will open this book. I won't be able to read it, right? I have no idea what the cover says."

"You'll understand when you open the book," Jilly said.

"Before I do, though, I want to know *what* are the Wraith-sworn and Elder-sworn. What the hell is out there?"

"Wraith-sworn are creatures sworn to the Wraiths," Jilly said with a shrug. "There in the name. The Wraiths are a species of beings not unlike the Wraiths of Earth myth."

"Ghosts?"

"Not quite. But close. Spirit beings. That bring destruction and despair. Dark entities. The, for want of a better word, demons sworn to the Wraiths carry out the destruction, foment the despair, and do the Wraiths' bidding in all things. They look like Wraiths. Insubstantial but deadly. Nothing to be underestimated."

"And the Elder-sworn, I assume, are creatures sworn to do the bidding of the Elders?"

"Right you are," Jilly said, with a faint grin. "The Elders are more like what humans would think of as old gods. The destructive, selfish, chaotic gods of old, though. No kindness or compassion. No benevolence. Unless of course it serves their ends. And then their benevolence comes with a price. One no sane person wants to pay. They've been at war with the Wraiths for eternity."

"For real eternity, or eternity in that we just don't know how long because it's been going on for so long?"

"That last one. There's no record of the beginning except in fables and stories. No actual documentation from that start. For as long as beings have recorded things, the stories of the Wraith-Elder war have existed. There is no good side in that war either. Both sides are bad for most of the beings in all the realms of existence. They have no care for others, only their own ends matter to them."

"So, okay, that all sounds pretty horrible."

"They are. Horrible and dangerous. Which is why we guard this place so carefully." Something flashed in Jilly's eyes.

"What?" Erica asked. "What was that look?"

"I haven't been as careful as I should, and I've brought us to this dangerous precipice. I'm beating myself up over it." She snorted and rolled her eyes.

"Don't do that," Erica said. Because she realized the

entire reason Jilly hadn't shown her this before was so that she could pursue her own dreams. Jilly had risked what she considered the fate of the world to let Erica have a life.

Jilly waved away her concern. "Water under the bridge, past is past, all the old clichés. We're here now. And all I need, all we need, is for you to open the book and begin your learning. That will solidify the transition, and that will thwart the Wraith-sworn."

"All right, then." Erica set a hand to the huge black book, just under the embossed writing she couldn't read. It was cool and soft under her fingers, the leather supple, the scents of ink and leather even stronger.

A shout from across the room, near the front of the temple made her drop her hand.

"Jilly," one of the women warriors said.

Athena or Morgaine? The woman was tall as Jilly and had white-blond hair against very dark brown skin. The coloring reminded Erica most of Morgaine, but probably she needed to get introduction to the others and who they were in their cat forms.

"They're at the door," the woman said. "They're trying to force their way inside."

"Damn it." Jilly faced Galahad. "Stay with her." To Erica. "Open the book, let it begin teaching you. Do *not* stop until it lets you go. Do you understand? No matter what happens, do *not* stop this initial reading." She pulled her sword from the scabbard and settled her shoulders. "Memnon?"

"I'm at your back," the man said, his voice a rumble as he also pulled his sword.

"Wait…" Erica started toward her aunt as she stalked back toward the front of the temple, but Galahad stopped her with a hand on her arm.

"You have to do as she said. If you don't, the Wraith-sworn will kill her."

"What?" Erica's voice rose a full octave. "I have to help her."

"You can only help her by doing as she said. Open the book. Learn to read it."

"I…" Erica swallowed hard, watched her aunt disappear behind the false wall that blocked her view of the temple entrance.

"Open the book, Erica," Galahad said quietly. "I'll keep you safe. Open the book."

Gut churning with fear, Erica set a hand to the book again. With a last glance toward the temple entrance, she pulled in a deep breath…

And opened the giant book.

CHAPTER 5

For a moment after opening the book, a strange kind of silence descended inside the temple, as if everything, everywhere was holding its breath.

Erica looked down at the pages. They were surprisingly white, not the crinkled yellow of age she'd been expecting. The pages smelled new too. No dusty, flaking scent. A fresh opened package of copy paper more like. And the ink smelled fresh too. Just laid down, but strong like someone had put a pen right under her nose. The ink was black, but might have been blue as well. The way it flickered in the light glowing from the temple stones made it impossible for her to really tell. Dark ink, though. A dark color against the thick, white paper. No bleed through effects on the page she'd opened.

The words—were they words?—were indecipherable to her. Symbols and forms that didn't coincide with the alphabet she knew. There was a circle in the center of the page, separated into four quadrants, each filled with what to her looked like drawings. A maze in one. A tree in another. Abstract shapes that seemed to be birds. And a starburst sort of image in the fourth. But all of the lines of the images were made up of symbols, sentences, maybe whole paragraphs twisted and curved to making the pictures. She leaned down to get a closer look, fascinated by the idea that someone had written a story into the image itself. That the image itself, composed of these words, *was* the story.

What kind of story? What did it say? Was it a history? A fiction? Fascinated, she traced the air over the images, following the lines as if reading them. If she could learn to read the images, learn to *know* them… What would she learn? What could she see?

Around the circle, more writing, laid out in columns and looking more familiar, filled in the rest of the page. The entire page was covered in ink, but the flow of it and shape of it seemed to carry meaning. If she could just grasp it…

The moment seemed to draw out for an eternity. Like she had all the time in the world to really sink into this new book and see where it led her.

Until a screeching wail filled the inside of the temple.

A howl of outrage so loud, so near, so sharp, Erica instinctively covered her ears and ducked, looking overhead for the attacker. Galahad stepped closer to her back, and she realized he was staring at the entrance of the temple.

The wailing went on and on, Erica's ears ringing with it as it echoed through the cavernous room, bouncing off books and shelves and stone walls, none of it absorbed into the surroundings. In fact, it seemed to grow louder, so loud Erica started to see spots.

Galahad's hands came up to her shoulders, holding her up, when her knees wobbled. "Concentrate on the book," he said near her ear, though she barely heard him over the wailing. "Turn the pages. Watch the ink."

"I can't read this." She nodded to the book because she didn't dare take her hands off her ears. Even though that thin protection wasn't doing much, she was afraid of what would happen if her ears were exposed to that sound without any dampening.

She realized Galahad, with his cat hearing, didn't have any barrier between him and the screech, and she wondered how his ears weren't bleeding.

"You don't have to read it," he said, again near her covered ear. "Just look, watch, see it. Study it. The understanding will come. Things will start to make sense the longer you study."

"They need help." This time she nodded toward the front of the temple.

His grin was so fast and startling she blinked. Had she seen the man that was Galahad grin before this?

"They've got this," he said. "Your aunt is the fiercest warrior I know."

The fact that she was supposed to take over for her aunt wasn't lost on Erica. She wasn't a fierce warrior. She wasn't a guardian of any kind. She was just an assistant history professor in Chicago whose allergies kicked up when the Chicago winds got going. She was an ordinary woman. And there was no way she was up for guarding this library and keeping anyone from invading and starting a war that would end her reality.

Panic clenched her throat. She couldn't do this. She wasn't the one. Her aunt was wrong. She would fail and everything would be destroyed.

The screech got louder, the wailing a knife in her skull. She couldn't read the words on the page in front of her. But the wailing, those were words in her head. She would fail. She couldn't do this. This was the end and everyone she knew would die.

Galahad's hands tightened on her shoulders and he leaned

into her back, warm and solid. "Look at the page, Erica. Your eyes are closed. Look at the page."

What? She hadn't realized she'd closed her eyes. The anguish of failure swamped her. The horror of what would happen filled her with so much gut-wrenching despair she could barely breathe around it. But she forced her eyes opened, forced herself to look at the book.

The images inside the circle moved. The order was different now. The starburst in the upper right corner now instead of the lower left. The tree now just above the starburst. The maze in line with the abstract birds. And as she watched, the lines inside the images moved, too. The words themselves marching along like tiny bugs. She leaned closer, staring harder.

What the…?

That was the weirdest thing she'd ever seen. Ink moving. Words moving. She stuck her nose right into the book, getting as close to the ink as possible. Was it bugs? But no. The words themselves were moving. They flowed like water across the shapes of the images. She blinked and they stopped moving. Words in her own alphabet and her own language, popped out of the image now. Not all of the writing was in her alphabet, and not all of the words in her alphabet were in her language, but certain words were, and they jumped out of the page almost like a 3D effect.

Life.

Hope.

Story.

Erica straightened a little. Wow. That was…wild.

She frowned down at the book, looking closer. Grinning when the word Cat jumped out at her. And then she spotted the word Love and her mind immediately went to her aunt. The thought of her aunt at the entrance, facing whatever was there, had her gut tightening in worry again. She started to look up from the book. But then another word jumped out of the image.

Destiny. She snorted. Destiny. Her aunt had called this her destiny. She had serious doubts her aunt knew what she was talking about.

Another word. Triumph.

Huh. What the hell story was written in this book?

Her curiosity about the story in front of her, what it was saying that she couldn't yet read… It reminded her of sifting through the rare documents about everyday life in different periods of time. Her work in grad school on the role of the book in the lives of Renaissance Europeans. Was this a story written about large things, big events. Destiny. Was it written by the powerful? Or was it about ordinary people, daily life? Was it a combination of those things? Fiction or history?

She leaned even closer to the book.

She dropped her hands from her ears to touch the image. Nothing moved under her fingers. That was both a surprise and a relief. She'd been anticipating a buggy feel of the ink crawling under her skin. But no, the images remained still. The ink didn't smudge either. Given it had been flowing just moments ago, the solidity of it on the page was pretty impressive. A few more words jumped out at her. Sun. Cosmos. She'd bet there was something really good in all this, some story she'd really enjoy if she could just…get it out, just decipher it.

She braced one hand against the table holding the book stand and flipped the page with her other. The new page held a lot more writing around another circle filled with images in the four quadrants, images drawn using tiny words instead of lines. So cool. She focused on the circle images, and another few words jumped out at her. Box. Box? What did that have to do with cosmic wars and cats? Well, she supposed cats did like boxes?

That idea made her chuckle under her breath even as she picked up a few more words. Paper. Rainbow. Fire.

The words felt random but they were part of sentences which meant that somewhere in there was the story. Somewhere in all that was a thing that made sense. She ran her finger across the lines, pausing whenever a word she could read jumped off the page.

She'd flipped through three more pages, picking up random words here and there, studying the images drawn inside each of the circles, when she suddenly realized…

The temple was silent.

The howling wail had stopped. Erica's ears were no longer ringing. Her brain wasn't full of despair and that torturous sense of failure. She wasn't on the verge of curling up into a ball and accepting that the universe was doomed.

She straightened away from the book and looked around.

Galahad was still behind her, his gaze intent on her, no sign of that quick grin he'd flashed earlier, but he didn't look upset either. She couldn't really read his expression. He just looked very focused. On her.

Then she noticed her aunt and the others were back, all standing around the table where she'd been studying the book. All of them just…staring at her.

Having all those cats' eyes focused on her was more than a little disconcerting.

"What's happening?" she asked, her gaze jumping from one person to the other, before she focused on Jilly. "What's going on?"

Jilly pulled in a deep breath that expanded her chest

before she let it out slowly. And then she smiled. "First steps," she said. "The beginning has begun."

"More cryptic talk? I do not need more cryptic from you today, Aunt Jilly."

Her smile turned into a chuckle. "The Wraith-sworn are gone for now. They didn't stop you. Your feet are now on the path."

"They'll be back," the man that was Memnon said from beside Jilly. "They always return. They'll test, and they'll keep trying to break through."

"But the new…guardian has started her training," Jilly said. "And that gives us some breathing room."

"I missed something, didn't I?" Erica looked closer at those surrounding her. No one was breathing hard, something she might have expected after a fight. So maybe they hadn't been in a physical fight after all? But then she realized that Memnon's shirt sleeve was ripped down its entire length. And Jilly had a cut on her cheek. The cut wasn't bleeding, but the sight of the injury brought Erica from behind the book. "You're hurt! Let me look at that."

Jilly waved her away. "A scratch." She glanced at the people around her. "I'm used to that." The human-cat-guards all chuckled. "I'll clean it out when we get back to my house."

"We get to go back, then, right? I mean… I don't live here now?"

"Of course not." Jilly's grin flashed. "There's no toilet here."

"Well that's not good."

"You'll come here regularly to study, to learn. To train. And in between the training, you'll continue with your life. Continue to work. Live. This will take time, and it needs to be a focus. This isn't something you can delay or put off." Jilly sighed. "I did too much of that for you already, I'm afraid. But you'll still be able to live in our world and do the work you love. You'll just need to do this as well."

Erica thought of her current schedule, of the work she did, classes she taught, the research she was in the middle of, the meetings and office hours and push to get her next paper finished. Adding one more thing to that, to the work she loved, wasn't going to be easy.

But was it that different? Another kind of research. A history very few people even knew. All at her fingertips to explore. To study. Could she do that at the same time as she maintained her regular life?

"What if I can't do it all?" she asked, quietly.

Jilly let out another long breath. "We'll deal with that if it happens. This isn't a duty you can neglect. But we'll find a way."

Erica looked down at the book again.

The images inside the circle began to move again, the words that made up the lines flowing until she felt like she could *almost* understand, *almost* see the story.

Could she do this? Could she at least try?

"At the very least," she said, her gaze on the book, "I'd love to know what the hell this book is saying. This story… seems good."

"Learning to read that story is just the start," Jilly said. "Once you get the hang of all this—" she gestured to the stacks of books, "—then you'll move on to the next steps. To retrieving books with the librarian and the others. Galahad will start your training in that aspect of the duty."

Erica glanced up at Galahad. He held her gaze, but didn't show a reaction to Jilly's comment. Just stared at her as she stared back. For some reason, the idea of working closely with Galahad left her a little nervous and jumpy. It was a reaction she'd have to analyze later.

"And I'll start your training with Alendrial when we're sure you're ready. She's more than just a sword, if you hadn't noticed, and she's integral to your work here."

Erica looked at the sword pommel sticking out from the scabbard at Jilly's hip. Learning to use a sword seemed… Well, kind of fun. But learning everything the sword could do was even more intriguing.

"There's time now," Jilly said. "For all of it."

The cat's eye jewel in the center of her diadem brightened, catching Erica's gaze. She stared at the jewel as the jewel seemed to stare back. The long dark center of the golden stone flickered, as if winking at her. Erica's brows rose. That was a trick of the light. It had to be.

But when she met Jilly's gaze again, prepared to ask, Jilly's grin stopped her.

"There's a lot to learn," Jilly said. "But when you're ready, when the time is right…" She touched the diadem, her fingers hovering near the jewel. "I will be happy, and proud, and relieved, to have you assume this work. You'll make an excellent guardian, love."

"You hope," Erica said, her worry leaking out into her voice.

"No," Jilly said. "This morning, I hoped." She glanced down at the book, then up at Erica again. "Now, I know."

Erica wasn't so sure Jilly knew what she was talking about. But when she glanced back down at the book, a few more words jumped out at her. Capturing her curiosity. Making her want to read more. Bottle. Pan. Home.

Home.

"And now it's time to go home," Jilly said, as if she'd

seen the word jump out from the page, too. "Home for a feast and some well-earned down time."

"And maybe a few more questions answered?"

Jilly grinned. "Probably. And then tomorrow, we'll come back. And the real learning will begin."

They returned to the temple entrance, Erica glancing around, almost reluctant to leave all this behind. She supposed that was a good sign.

"How will I get back and forth?" she asked as they stepped back out into the giant forest. To Erica's surprise, it was dark now, the sky overhead black and sprinkled with stars so bright they lit up the clearing around the temple.

Jilly pulled out her sword, the steel glowing that luminous blue that lit the darkness as they headed back down the forest path. "You'll have a cat tree of your own," she said. "In fact, it should be finished by the time you get home."

"Finished?" Erica stumbled and Galahad caught her elbow, keeping her from falling. Again. She flashed him an embarrassed thanks before focusing more closely on the path in front of her. It was easier to see her way than she'd expected. So long as she concentrated.

"The tree…builds itself. It'll be waiting for you."

"Won't that look weird? Me having a cat tree and no cats?"

Without looking back, Jilly said, "Oh, you'll have one cat. You'll need a guard of your own. And someone who can help you navigate all this while you're learning to balance this duty and your daily life."

"Who?" Erica asked, but a part of her already knew. She looked back and met Galahad's gaze. He'd avoided her for as long as she'd known him.

"Galahad, of course. He's your librarian. And one of your teachers."

Now he couldn't avoid her anymore. She raised her brows at him. He stared back without comment.

"As a cat?" she asked.

"Most of the time," he said, his voice deep in the darkness under the trees. "But I won't be…restricted to that form in your realm anymore."

"Mm hmm." She turned back toward Jilly, following in silence for a moment before saying, "Am I going to end up the cat lady with a clowder of cats that are actually warrior-guard-librarians?"

"Once you have one warrior-guard-librarian cat, I'm afraid more just show up." Jilly chuckled. "It's not a bad way to live, love. You'll see."

Erica wasn't sure how to feel about all this. But for reasons she couldn't really explain to herself, she wasn't as upset about it all as she'd have assumed. It was definitely going to take some getting used to.

She looked at Jilly's back as she marched through the trees, a glowing blue sword over her head, surrounded by her clowder. Then she glanced back at Galahad.

Protecting the knowledge of the universe, saving the world from a cosmic war, learning a lot of history she hadn't dreamed of before, her own personal clowder of guardian cats led by Galahad…

Her aunt might be right.

Maybe this wouldn't be a bad way to live after all.

THE UNSHATTERED SWORD

CHAPTER 1

The fire crackled gently in the giant open fireplace next to her seat as she stared at the hard, gray flagstone floor. The scent of peat filled the spacious, airy room, mixing with a soft, damp loamy smell filtering in through the opened windows. Despite the glass panes being pushed back, allowing the dawn in, the room was warm. Maybe too warm, but that hardly mattered now.

Not with the fate of her people resting on her shoulders.

Soft velvet curtains hung solid, unmoving despite the open windows. No breeze this early in the morning. Everything had stilled and settled. Unlike her heartbeat. The point was to settled herself. The privacy. The quiet. This time alone without the others. She was supposed to be settling and preparing. All she felt was the rapid thump of her heartbeat. The hard support of her wooden chair despite the generous cushions covering the base and back. The heavy weight of her leather armor on top of her thin, cotton underclothes.

So much depended on her. On this day. On her strength.

They'd brought her a feast of course. There was always a feast the night before. Roasted meats and fowl, smoked river fish, vegetables prepared with buttery sauces, thick slabs of bread and honey, rich pastries filled with sugared fruits and topped with thickened cream. Plenty of drink too. Caskets and barrels of beer and wine. Flowing freely through the dining hall below and in the village surrounding the stone keep. That was good for others. To dull the fear. Her flagon of wine remained untouched. She'd drink it if they survived the day. And if they didn't…

Well, it was good wine. The best her people made. Someone else would likely drink it. Or toss it onto the flames of her clan.

All of that depended on today. Who was the strongest. Who could overcome their strongest.

Whether or not they could get through her.

The heavy oak door eased gently open as her second came into the room. Eian was older than her by several decades, and not able for the coming fight any more for reasons no one discussed, but he'd been a reassuring presence as she'd trained and prepared. A mentor of sorts, though not her teacher. Twenty years ago, he'd been the one to stand before the army. Now it was her turn. And having his experience at her back brought more comfort than she could offer in return.

He'd bathed recently. His dark, steal gray hair was still damp, the tiny braids through the top holding his thick mane back from his strong, wide face, the ends of his hair curling around the raised collar of his leather jerkin. Later, he'd strap his short sword to his hip. Mostly for show.

No one fought except her.

And the Gastion's Champion.

"Are you ready, Lilia?" Eian's voice was deep and rumbling in the large space, quiet but still managing to boom despite his best efforts. No one in the entire community had a voice like his.

He held up the long sword he'd brought into the room, the blade pulled just a little from its scabbard, the weapon resting across his spread hands.

Uniquely forged for the battle to come. The double-edged blade made of silver, etched with ancient runes. Purple gems decorated the knotted silver pommel. The grip wrapped in hardened purple leather. The cross-guard spread in a wide T shape, the ends curving down and molded to resemble ancient monsters. A swirling, knotted silver designs decorated the top of the leather scabbard.

The Champion's sword.

Standing, moving to face Eian, she took the sword from him, holding it as he had across her palms. Staring at it for a long moment.

"Are you ready, Lilia?" he asked again.

I settled the strap of the scabbard over my head, letting it fall across my back, feeling the weight of the sword on my shoulders.

I smiled. Feeling the smile. Not having to fake it. "I'm ready."

My palms sweated. My heartbeat hammered. My stomach clenched.

But I was ready.

I would not let my people down.

CHAPTER 2

The battlefield spread out before us, a huge, open expanse of grasslands, the rough green carpet damp with dawn dew. The Gastion stood across the wide-open field, arrayed in tight lines, so many warriors in silver armor glinting brightly in the early morning light. Mist spilled out of the thick forest behind them, but the field on which they would battle had cleared. The morning would be cool and bright.

A good day to die, Eian would say.

I wouldn't let that happen.

The leaders of our two people rode out first, to the center of the field. The Gastion ruler, a powerful woman in her prime, rode a large bay stallion, holding the massive beast under control with impressive ease as it danced under her. Even with her silver armor, her seat looked relaxed, her hands on the reins steady and low.

Our leader, Bastia MacMoor, was also an impressive sight upon their black horse, another huge stallion whose manner was less excitable than the Gastion ruler's horse. The MacMoor rode looser limbed, their leather armor revealing their posture and demeanor more fully than the Gastion's silver armor. Done to intimidate. The MacMoor hadn't even bothered with chainmail or extra weaponry. They didn't even have their sword as they rode to the center of the open grass. Nothing but themselves and their army behind them.

And me.

The Gastion ruler, whose name I refused to think or speak, raised her arm overhead. A bright blue glow rose up her arm, coalescing in the palm of her hand until the sphere was the size of her own steed's head.

"Let the battle commence." Her voice boomed across the open field like lightning and thunder. She dropped her arm and the blue sphere flashed into the ground, spreading out in a circle of power, moving so fast it washed over both armies in moments, extending to the very back of each. Closing in the battlefield.

No one would run away now. No one could retreat. We were locked on this field.

Until someone was victorious.

The MacMoor nodded their head, a small smile played over their mouth. "Our champion is ready." Their voice boomed less, but carried just as well across the open space. Impossible to ignore the confidence, the ease. "Is yours?" the MacMoor asked, smirking at their rival ruler.

I hoped I could live up to their confidence.

If I failed, it meant the destruction of my people. The Gastion would roll across our lands, take as they pleased, and we would have to step aside and allow it. So went the rules of combat in this section of Faery. Too much magic let loose in a Fae war could destroy everyone, everything. This way of battle, this ancient tradition, was the only thing that kept warring factions from tearing the realm down to its knees.

And the responsibility for everything now sat with me.

The MacMoor's armor now danced with a bluish purple light, their magic building and encircling them, a glittering shimmer of light to remind the Gastion ruler that our people were not the weak clan the Gastion assumed. The purple-blue light traveled into the MacMoor's dark brown hair, sparking in little electrical jolts over the jewelry woven into their braids, across their dark skin, lighting up their purple eyes in a way that was visible to both armies. Truly, the MacMoor was an impressive sight. If only the leaders were the champions, no one would doubt the MacMoor's strength of will.

But the rulers weren't allowed to take the field as champion. By law and tradition, it had to be one of their people.

This time, it had to be me.

From the Gastion army, a large man stepped out onto the field. He was easily seven foot tall, with shoulders as wide as a spreading oak. He wore a silver breast shield over his leathers, the symbol of the Gastion—an oak leaf on a circular field—embossed in gold on the center. But that was his only concession to armor. He had a sword strapped to his hip, the long sword in that position ensured the man looked impressively tall in comparison. His long blond hair was pulled away from his face into a single braid, with glinting, multicolored stones decorating the golden plait.

His dark-eyed gaze found me across the field, though I hadn't stepped away from my army yet. He smiled. I didn't return the gesture. I didn't show any expression at all.

At a subtle hand gesture from the MacMoor, and a quiet word from Eian, I finally moved away from my army, stepping out in front of them.

And pulled my sword from its scabbard across my back.

The sound of the silver blade running against the

decorative silver at the top of my scabbard sent a shiver down my spine. The noise was loud. Obvious in the clearing. Even with the giant armies at my back and before me. Thousands strong each. Yet silent. The sound of my sword coming free heard clearly over that silence.

The Gastion champion pulled his sword, another rub of silver against silver. Clear and full of foreboding.

No steal or iron alloys here in Faery. Most of us, even the high Fae, couldn't stand the touch of iron. But we had other ways of making metals we could tolerate into strong and functional weaponry. The army behind me mostly carried bow and arrow, the arrows tipped with glass sharp flint arrowheads. Some carried shorter silver daggers. Very few, like Eian, had full swords. Their chainmail was also made of silver or gold, strengthened into protective armor with magic, just like the swords.

The army behind the Gastion's champion was the same. Those arrows were the weapons to fear, though. The arrows were the entire problem. One of the reasons this type of combat had developed.

When the rulers of our two clans separated and turned back toward their armies, the Gastion champion and I moved farther forward. The MacMoor gave me a nod as they passed, their black steed steady and solid beneath them. I bowed my head in respect until they were past. A fleeting glance confirmed the Gastion's ruler had rejoined her army as well, her battle steed continuing to dance beneath her with restless energy.

Then my gaze settled on the enemy champion. This was it. The time had come. And everything depended on this one fight.

We crossed to the center of the field, remaining several hundred yards distance from one another as we assessed each other. Could I stand strong against him? Could I take the best the Gastion had in this moment? Could he take the best my people had?

I raised my sword first, high overhead, the tip toward the sky. Purple lightning raced down the length of the silver blade, spiking from the clear sky into my sword. I held the Gastion's gaze as he brandished his own sword. More purple lightning pulled from the surrounding magic, filling our weapons. Filling us.

I swung the sword back, circling it over my hand into a firm grip, took it in two hands with the tip now pointing at the ground, and drop to my knees, driving the sword deep into the earth. Waves of magic rippled from the contact, a rock into a pond. I stood, letting the sword remain where it was, and spread my hands wide.

Extending my magical shield.

The Gastion did the same, driving his sword into the earth, widened his stance, spread his fingers…

And the first volley of arrows filled the clear sky.

I concentrated on the arrows coming from the enemy, throwing my hands higher to ensure the shield kept my people safe. Watching the arrows slam into the shimmering air where my shield was, feeling the bubble of its magic in my blood, I let out a slow breath when each arrow hit the shield, each deadly little missile smashed against my magic…

And didn't continue through.

The arrows clattered on top of each other until there was a layer of wood and flint hovering above my army. I sent a ripple of motion through the shield, and the now harmless arrows jumped and scattered to one side of the field. I didn't have a chance to check on the results of the volley against the Gastion. Another wave of deadly arrows whistled above. I raised my arms again, blocking the next attack successfully, keeping my people safe.

An injury wouldn't end the battle. But a death, one death, any death would. The champion who failed, who couldn't keep their people protected from enemy fire, lost the fight. Losing the fight meant losing everything and becoming subjects of our enemies. Subject to their whims and cruelties. Even their benevolence wouldn't be enough to counter the destruction to our clan. The Gastion outnumbered us, three to one. We would eventually cease to be if I lost this fight.

I couldn't lose.

The second volley of arrows met the same fate as the first, a pile of now useless wood at the side of the battlefield. I let out another breath and rolled my shoulders.

The next volley wasn't made with arrows. Now came the magic, the spells, the power.

First a sphere of blue magic slammed against my shield, spreading in a wave of licking electrical lines across my protective powers, searching for an opening, a weakness. I firmed my stance and spread my arms out to the sides as I widened my shield, ensured it moved higher overhead.

I could extend the shield only so far. There were limits to what I could do. Limits to what the Gastion could do. That was the point. Who had the better shield. Who could keep everything the enemy threw at you out.

A flicker of the lines dancing over my shield to my right had me gasping, and I quickly threw a second shield up to block the sneaking magic. Holding more than one shield was always harder, dividing the magic into multiple layers to keep more sections of the army safe risked weakening the overall effect of each shield.

More magic flew at me. This from the leader herself. The Gastion ruler would be the most powerful magic wielder among her people. It was the only way to lead and remain in that position among the Fae. The MacMoor was our greatest wielder of magic as well. And when they cast their first attack, the enemy champion's shield trembled.

He swung his hand in an arc and the visible blue of his

shield strengthened, flickering here and there before solidifying. The MacMoor's attack didn't get through.

But seeing my opponent waiver under the onslaught from my people was heartening.

Another volley of arrows came toward us and all my concentration went to maintaining my defenses, holding the line. The attack intensified. More arrows, more magic from across their army. They had ten, twenty Fae with powerful magic, the kind of magic useful in a war. And they didn't pause as they sent those attacks to test my own protective powers.

My sword trembled where I'd buried it in the ground a few yards in front of me. More magic channeled from the sky and earth into the sword, then flowed into me.

The sword was the focus, the way of pulling magic from Faery itself to help aid the defensive magic I used. The Gastion champion's weapon was the same. His also drew that magic, strengthened his defenses. We were trained to be shields, to be defensive weapons. Our swords channeled the power we needed.

Seeing my sword vibrate with the magic I was drawing made my breath hitch. Fear? Uncertainty? Any of those would weaken my efforts. I dragged my gaze from the sword and focused on the increasing attack. Focused on just holding the shields. Still, with two instead of a single protective barrier, though, there were weaknesses in my defense. I needed to weave the two shields together.

But the enemy didn't give me time.

The Gastion ruler joined her powerful mages, pummeling me with blast after blast of magic. From her, there were no longer any attack spells, no spells at all. Just pure, unfiltered magic. Wave after wave of it. Attack after attack of power slamming into me. The rawness of it, the strength, made my knees trembled. Slid me backward a few steps across the wet grass.

I braced my legs to hold steady and forced my arms higher, readjusting my shields to take all that power.

The pummeling made my shoulders ache. My arms shiver. I widened my stance so I wouldn't fall to my knees. More power. More raw magic. No time to strengthen the two shields, to tie them together into a stronger barrier.

Gasping against the powerful attack, I tried to meld the two shields even as I used them to keep my people covered, but the power I was pulling through my buried sword from Faery itself, as well as what I drew from my own strength and inner resources, all of it was weakening. I could feel it. Feel the thinness of my barrier, tiny holes opening up.

From behind me, I was vaguely aware of my own people countering the attack, throwing all they had back at the Gastion's shield. But I didn't dare pay too much attention to what they were doing. All my concentration was on my defenses, defenses that weren't strong enough, on the tremor racing through my muscles, making it harder to hold the shields up.

I felt more than saw the barrier shrinking toward me. Not enough power in it. Not enough skill. I dug deeper, pushed harder against the attack, dragged more power from the sword. I needed more. This wasn't enough. I needed more.

Beneath me the ground shivered.

My sword waved like a thin tree caught in a gale.

Then a flickering to my left... My breath caught. A weakness in my defense, a tiny gap in between the two shields. Barely there. But there long enough...

An arrow flew through the hole. Toward my people.

Physical shields came up but they weren't a match to the

magic tipping these arrows, and the arrow pierced through several of them before burying into the ground.

One person held her arm as drips of blood fell from her wounded shoulder. But no one lay dead.

The wounded Fae, Immogen, waved away my terrified gaze, my silent question, assuring me she was fine. I let out a long breath, though I couldn't relax my clenched teeth. I'd nearly failed. Nearly allowed someone to die.

We'd almost lost everything.

That terror would consume me and weaken my shield. The terror and the fear. I had to overcome it. That was the battle. The fight.

But I couldn't. Everything in me clenched and tightened and the fear of what had nearly happened overwhelmed me. A terror greater than facing my own death. Knowing I was responsible for the loss of one of my people, that I couldn't protect them…

No. I couldn't lose one. I couldn't lose a single person.

I would not let that happen.

The arrows flew, even as I poured my determination, my terror into my shield. I dragged more and more power through my sword, filtering it into my own power, using it to reinforce my shield. I started pulling from my inner magic stronger, everything I had went into strengthening my protections. Making sure none of my people were harmed. I no longer paid attention to what was happening with the Gastion champion because all my focus was on my sword, on building a stronger and stronger shield.

The sword continued to vibrate where it was imbedded in the ground, the thin blade waving, bending. Bending toward me. Almost as if I were pulling the sword toward me as I drew more and more power through it.

A line of visible magic now flowed through the hilt,

powered into me, coming from the very foundations of Faery. I dragged it all into me, every last bit, all of it channeled into the shields.

And then, to my horror…

The sword shattered.

CHAPTER 4

*S*plintered into a thousand sharp shards, flung across the grass in a glittering confetti of disaster. A howl of destruction rent the air, like the physical scream of a creature dying.

The Champion's sword.

Gone.

For a moment, an instant, everything seemed to stop. The world. Time. My breath.

In that still and silent moment, I knew my shield would also shatter. That it would crumble without the sword. The sword was the source… Not of the magic but of the shield. The filter through which the magic was channeled to build the shield. Without it…

My people were dead.

But I couldn't allow that. I was the shield. I was their defense. I couldn't let them down. I refused to let even one die.

I pulled in a breath, what felt like my first in an eternity, and then I pulled in more magic. No longer filtered through the sword. Directly from Faery now, from the air, from the sky, from inside me. From everything around me. I pulled in all the magic I could hold. It gathered in my chest and gut, bubbled in my blood.

And I poured that into the shield.

A pulse of purple light, bright enough to make me squint, grew and sparkled around me, iridescent as a pearl.

I continued to pull strength from the very soil beneath my feet, from the essence of Faery itself. The power filled me to bursting and I knew it was too much. Without the sword to filter it, it was too much. But I couldn't stop. I didn't dare let anything else through. Not now that the sword was gone. I had to be the sword.

And I would not break.

Taking in more and more, all I could manage. Pouring all that power into my shield. The shimmering, purple light of my shield pulsed, brightened, grew more and more opaque, until I could no longer see the enemy army, or their arrows. There was no sense of place, no sense of time. Just the magic pouring into me, through me, channeled into my protections. Knowing I had to keep my people safe. Knowing I couldn't stop.

And even as I pulled in more power, I felt my body pushed too far. Too much. I had taken in too much. Absorbed it without using it. So I sent more of it into the shield. And more. Letting it expand forward, backward, encircling my people now, not just shielding them from the front.

Over the sounds of blood roaring in my ears, I heard someone shout. I couldn't tell who. My people? One of the Gastion?

Did it matter now?

Part of me sensed the continued attack beyond my shield, the glowing heat of other magic slamming against the barrier, the ping of wickedly tipped arrows. Nothing got through. Nothing came close.

Still the power filled me. Still too much.

I poured more into the shield and let it expand farther. A space of fresh air and loamy earth opened up around me. The bitter electric flavor of active magic cleared from my mouth. More shouting I couldn't decipher. More magic flowing through me, from the land around me, and into my shield.

I took a deep breath, let it out slowly through my mouth, surprised I could still breathe. When was my last breath? That air felt good. Tasted like life. I needed more.

Another slow breath. And when I breathed out, I pushed my shield out farther too. Letting it take up more space, giving me more room. And then again, more space, more air, more shield.

Oh the fresh air. The clearness. I blinked open my eyes, though I hadn't realized I'd closed them, and looked around. The shield had pushed out far enough to encompass the shattered pieces of my sword. It filled the sky in a solid dome of protection over my people. At some point I had dropped my arms to my sides, no longer physically holding the shield up. Magic pulsed from me, and with each pulse a visible wave of light moved through the shield.

The sight of it was mesmerizing. Thoughts of the attack beyond the shield faded. Nothing would get through this. We were safe. My people were safe. I could stand here, just like this, holding this powerful protection from now to eternity. I felt that in my bones, my bubbling blood. I could breathe. Magic continued to pour through me, meeting no resistance, and flowing into the shield. I wasn't sure I could stop the flow of magic, but I didn't want to. Not yet. My people were safe. So I would channel the magic until I couldn't anymore.

I felt more than saw the MacMoor move up beside me,

but I continued to stare at the shield, as if looking away might shatter my connection to it, break apart whatever I was doing now to keep the magic flowing through me. Being the sword.

On my other side, Eian moved into my peripheral view. He was also staring up at the shield. "What have ye done?"

"I don't know," I murmured. My voice was raw and deep and gravely. Not my usual voice. Barely recognizable.

"Your glowing?" Eian said, also quietly.

"The magic." Of course it was the magic. All of it. Flowing through me. I couldn't see it, didn't dare look down yet. But…

But I felt in control of what I was doing now. Was I? Could I stem the flow? Could I stop channeling all this magic without destroying the shield?

Without destroying me?

"What's happening with the enemy?" I asked.

The MacMoor answered. "They've ceased their attack."

"Have we won?"

Silence. No answer.

Then, "No one on their side has died either," Eian said.

The "either" in that sentence was a relief. That meant none of our people had been killed. Though I knew my shield had been protecting everyone, a small part of me worried that something could have snuck through.

"Can we call a truce? An end?"

"How long can you hold this shield?" the MacMoor asked.

"Forever." I wasn't exaggerating. I felt like I could stand here until the end times. Until the fall of Faery. As more and more magic from Faery poured through me, I was no longer afraid of it killing me. It felt…right that I was the conduit. Nothing more. Nothing less. A channel for magic outside myself, all of it going to protect my clan.

"Without the sword," Eian said.

He wasn't asking me a question. His was a statement of fact. I was doing this without any barrier between me and the magic. No longer in need of a funnel for that power. A direct conduit. Without need of an object to focus and concentrate the protective spells.

"Can you stop?" the MacMoor asked.

And there I heard their worry, the slight tremor in their voice.

"I can," I told them with as much surety as I could manage, my deep and gravely voice adding something stronger to the statement.

My skin tingled all over from the flow of magic, but the sensation was lovely, like immersion in a bubbling hot spring. I hadn't experienced that since I was a youngling, but the sensory memory filled me then and I smiled. This felt good. I wouldn't break from it. I wouldn't shatter.

I barely felt like myself anymore, and yet I felt as if this was always me, always part of me. I was made to do this. To be this.

To *be* the shield.

"Then we've won," the MacMoor said. No more worry in their voice. Now just a fierce satisfaction.

They rode forward, to the edge of my shield, now almost the full length of the battlefield.

I blinked when I realized how far out I'd extended the barrier without realizing it.

When the MacMoor reached the edge of the barrier, I sent a shimmer of power through it, not enough to drop it, but to clear the solid opaqueness of it. The purple faded in a single spot before the MacMoor, but the visible sparkle of my magic remained.

They glanced back at me once before facing forward

again. Their steed remained steady beneath them, despite the shimmer glimmer of the shield only a foot before the animal's nose.

On the opposite side, the Gastion ruler stood staring up at my shield. She was no longer on her horse, which was curious enough to draw a murmured remark from Eian.

"Do you yield?" the MacMoor asked, their voice loud enough to carry to both armies.

The Gastion ruler dropped her gaze to meet the MacMoor's. There was rebellion in her dark eyes. But resignation in her broad shoulders. Her silver armor, still shiny and bright, reflected the purple glow of my shield.

"I yield," she said, her voice also loud enough for both armies to hear. "The battle is won. The Gastion will cede the field.

I expected a yowl of protest from the Gastion. Some noise of dissent. No one had been killed. The single combat was a test of mine and the Gastion champion's defenses. Nothing had gotten through his defenses either. According to the rules of this single combat, no one had won yet.

But nothing was getting through my barrier. There was no way for the Gastion to win now. Only a way for them to lose. To continue the fight, meant it was only a matter of time before one of their people died.

The Gastion ruler declaring an end before that happened was…unexpected. But I had more respect for her now. She considered the lives of those she ruled, and didn't consider even one of them expendable. That was more than I'd expected from her.

"We are finished," she said, louder this time. "The truce will be negotiated on neutral ground. The terms to suit both peoples."

"With a little more for us," Eian whispered.

He was right. Though the battle was called, everyone here knew we had won. And the victors determined the terms of a settlement. If the MacMoor was wise—and I thought they were—the terms would be mutually beneficial, not too harsh on the Gastion. And we wouldn't have to battle again for several centuries.

Some more quiet conversation happened then, for the leaders' ears only. I didn't drop the shield between them, continuing to protect my people from any duplicitous acts from the Gastion. Even with a truce declared, I wouldn't trust the safety of my leader with the Gastion just yet.

When the MacMoor rode back to the army, I kept my attention on the Gastion ruler, visible through the window I'd created in the shield. She stared up at me for a long time, holding my gaze. She didn't snarl or show any obvious emotion at all. Just stared. I stared back.

She nodded once, her expression never changing, and turned her back to me. I had no idea what that exchange had meant. What any of this meant. But I wouldn't show my confusion in front of the enemy.

Or... Well, not friend yet. But maybe no longer enemy. For a time.

I didn't lower the shield until the MacMoor gave me a nod.

Then I let it collapse. Some of the power returned to me, settling into my blood as if it had always been there. Some of it washed out as a fresh breeze through the very air of Faery. Some bubbled into the ground like water sinking into the soil.

When it was gone, when I'd released all of the magic that had built into the shield, a rumble of thunder sounded in the distance.

An omen or a sign? I wasn't a seer. I had no way to know. But I took it as approval. Because no one had died this day.

Not even me.

The MacMoor gave me an approving nod before calling for the army to return to the keep. The sounds of marching emphasized the silence that had fallen. A quietness unusual to a victorious army. We would celebrate tonight. Another feast. More drink. Beer and wine. Maybe even mead. But for now, everything was murmurs and whispers and a deliciously fresh breeze blowing across my face.

"No one is cheering," I said to Eian.

"Too awed by what happened," he said. "So am I." He faced me. "Could you do it again?"

I nodded. "I'll have to experiment. Practice. But…yes. I could do this again."

"Hmm." He pursed his lips, rubbed at his jaw. "Hmm." Then he smiled. Just a little. And turned back toward the keep.

We walked side-by-side. Following the army.

Returning safely home.

CARY AT THE HAUNT AND HOWL

A CARY REDMOND SHORT STORY

Cary Redmond walked into the heat and swirling lights of the Haunt and Howl nightclub in downtown Portland with a mission. To help her best friend Marianne Johnson spy.

Marianne's girlfriend Gina had opened a new nightclub of her own a little over a year and a half ago. That nightclub had been Gina's dream for years and was the entire reason she and Marianne moved to Portland from New York City. So far, the club was doing pretty well. The Eighties Night Gina had started on Sundays to please Marianne—who, like Cary, was crazy about all things Eighties—had been a particular hit, drawing older and younger crowds a like. The older in particular proved profitable since they were the ones with money and they liked the more expensive alcohols.

And then the Haunt and Howl opened.

To be fair, there were a lot of nightclubs in Portland. Cary didn't know that much about the business, but she wouldn't have thought yet another opening wouldn't make all that much different. Gina's club was well established enough, with a pretty regular clientele. The new place shouldn't have impacted her.

Except Gina had seen a sharp drop in income and customers since the Haunt and Howl opened a few blocks from her club.

Again, that wouldn't necessarily have been nefarious. New attracted a lot of attention. Gina's own club had benefited from the "new" phenomena. It was sticking past the first few months that was important. Getting through the "new" period and becoming a regular for enough people. At least, that's what Marianne had told Cary.

But something about this particular club…

Marianne hadn't been able to explain it very well. She just said she thought something about the new place was… off. Off in a way that was more a part of Cary and Marianne's worlds than Gina's.

Gina was mundane and had no idea that things like werewolves and vampires and Fae and the occasional demon walked the earth. She had no idea her girlfriend was a magical weaver—Marianne could so some truly amazing things with needle and thread—or that one of her girlfriend's best friends was a magical Protector. But Marianne knew exactly what kinds of strange things lurked in the world. So when she called asking Cary for help, help that required Cary's particular set of skills, Cary couldn't refuse.

It had taken her and Marianne a good hour of waiting in a line to get inside the nightclub. Cary wasn't a waiting-in-line kind of person. She was not that patient. But she'd waited. For Marianne. Tapping her foot the entire time. Her only consolation was Marianne had let her get away with her normal clothes—jeans, a t-shirt, hiking boots, and her leather jacket. If she'd had to stand that long in heels, she'd have been significantly more grumpy about the wait.

Her leather jacket was actually a Marianne creation with actual magic pockets that kept Cary's keys and wallet and phone from falling out when she had to dive around protecting good guys from bad guys. So even if she'd dressed up, she'd have worn that to the club. The jacket, and its magic pockets, was her favorite piece of clothing and she rarely went out without it.

Finally, finally after too long a wait, they were let through the ropes and into the light swirling heat of the interior club.

And boy was it hot. Sweltering. Surprisingly hot, giving it was early November and getting pretty chilly outside. Not cold enough yet to warrant heaters inside, though. Especially not with all the bodies packed so tightly into the club. In fact, what the place needed was a little air conditioning.

Cary adjusted her jacket, sweat dripping down her back, and blew out a breath that moved the hairs on her already sweaty forehead. Her ponytail felt sticky against the back of her neck, which didn't bode well for spending more time in the club.

Music pulsed so loudly she couldn't hear her own voice—techno music she vaguely associated with Europe even though she'd never been to Europe. The wooden floor vibrated beneath her. Bodies bounced and moved to the rhythm in a tight clench, making it difficult to navigate the space or even see very much of what was happening.

From her vantage in the middle of all those bodies, Cary got the impression of the club being a single large space. There didn't seem to be any other levels, just this single massive dance floor, no circling gallery overhead like in Gina's club. There weren't any visible stairs. But the ceiling with its exposed industrial beams and swirling, multi-colored lights was easily fifteen to twenty feet high. Lots of open space that still left her feeling a little claustrophobic because of all the people.

Marianne motioned her toward one side of the room and they pushed through the crowds, Cary in the lead because that's what Protectors did. Not that she actually knew what she might be protecting Marianne from. So far, the place seemed like an ordinary, if overly hot, nightclub in the midst of a very busy Friday night.

The music's deep base vibrated up from the floor and through her body, so Cary wasn't even sure she'd feel the tell-tale tingling along her spine that signaled her brand of help was needed. The one good thing about her magic, though, was that it just worked. She didn't have to know what danger was there. If there was danger, and she was standing between that danger and a good guy, her magic kept the good guy safe. No matter what the danger actually was—magic or mundane, shifter or mugger. Whatever might be a threat, Cary could keep people safe from it.

It wasn't actually, technically, *her* magic. She hadn't been born with it the way Marianne had been born a weaver. Cary had been "hired" to be a Protector. She even got paid, which was nice compensation considering she'd been tricked into the job. The magic that made up her Protector shield came from her Fae bosses, whom she'd nicknamed the Nags because they were. Cary just channeled their magic. But she channeled it well. Because, outside of the occasional bump or bruise when she had to dive between innocent people and bad guys at the last minute, the magic always worked and the good guys—if they *let* her protect them—didn't die.

Since Marianne knew how Cary's magic worked, she stayed behind Cary, gripping her leather jacket so they didn't get separated, letting Cary protect her from...

Well, whatever might turn up.

The too-loud music beat in Cary's pulse and left her edgy and uncomfortable. She wasn't opposed to loud music and nights at a club dancing until the sweat dripped. She liked those nights occasionally. She'd spent several nights doing exactly that with Marianne and her other friends at Gina's club. Just recently.

But something about this place was grating against Cary's nerves. She couldn't explain it any better than Marianne had been able to. Just that the music, the bodies, the musky smell of sweat and too many different kinds of perfumes, the *heat* set her teeth on edge.

After some maneuvering, pushing and shoving, they reached the bar. It was a long curved wooden counter backed by shelves of alcohol in sparkling glass bottles staged in front of a mirrored wall that made the alcohol look like it stretched back for a mile. The illusion was a little disorienting, so Cary ignored the wall as she pushed up to the counter. All the people around her were bouncing to the beat, even though they weren't on the dance floor, and the constant jostling did nothing to sooth her nerves.

Wow was this place irritating her. She had no idea why. It was just...crawling over her skin. Something about it really got her hackles up.

"What do you want?" she shouted over the noise to Marianne.

"Coke," Marianne shouted back. "No alcohol."

Since they were here to spy and not party, that sounded like a good plan. When her gaze skimmed over the wall of alcohol, and that disorienting feeling swept through her again, she decided a plain Coke would be best for her, too.

She pressed against the counter, going up on her toes to catch the bartender's attention. Two of them worked the crowd. An extremely tall, full-bodied woman, her thickly coiled braids twinned into a bun on top of her head, worked the far end of the long bar. And wow was that far. It must have been nearly the length of the entire place. Cary couldn't even really see the woman well she was so far away. The swirl of multi-colored lights made the woman appear to fade in and out of existence, too. Like she'd be in one spot, the lights would hide her for a second, and then she'd be in a completely different spot. Another illusion that made Cary's head spin.

She faced the bartender closer to her side of the counter, a man who was as tall as the woman, his thick beard and mustache dominated a face she couldn't otherwise see well in the flashing lights. He had broad shoulders, pulling tight against his buttoned up black dress shirt, and his hands were so big, they made the glasses and alcohol bottles look like kids' toys.

Both bartenders struck her as more front-door-bouncer size than behind-the-bar size, but maybe that was just coincidence. Or maybe the club hired bouncers who could also tend bar.

At any rate, getting the man's attention took her a good five minutes. She was about to give up, her impatience overwhelming her need to drink—despite the heat and sweat drying her throat—when the large man seemed to materialize out of the swirling lights right in front of her.

"What can I get you?" he asked. His voice wasn't as deep as she'd been expecting from his size, but it carried over the sound of the music in a remarkably easy way. No shouting or straining to hear him at all.

Maybe some trick of the bar setup ensured sound carried better here? Or…something.

Weird.

She shook off the creeping sense of unease to order two

sodas, holding up her fingers to indicate the number in case he couldn't hear her—she still had to shout over the noise and, at least to her own ears, it sounded like her voice was whisked away into the music's beat.

But he must have heard her clearly enough because a moment later, two tall, thin glasses filled with soda and ice and a single cherry plunked onto the counter in front of her.

"Twenty," the man said.

She gulped. Twenty bucks for two sodas. Not even very large sodas. How did anyone afford the alcohol?

Marianne passed him the cash past Cary's shoulder, along with another ten for a tip.

Cary stared at her. "Ten for a tip?" she asked.

Marianne shrugged. "Worth the good will," she said against Cary's ear so she'd be heard over the music without having to shout. "We're here to spy, remember. Better to keep the staff happy so they don't look at us too closely."

Cary thought a tip that size might do the exact opposite to making them blend in, but she kept that opinion to herself. Marianne knew more about the nightclub world than she did. Maybe a fifty percent tip was what it took to keep bartenders from noticing you.

She picked up her soda but didn't immediately gulp it down, despite her thirst, because a ten dollar soda seemed like it should last for longer than a minute. Then she scanned the crowd. They'd been there long enough that the song playing should have changed, but the beat still sounded the same to her. Like the song just went on and on and on. Probably just another illusion, the different songs having a similar beat so they seemed to blend together.

Leaning in close to Marianne, she said in her ear, "Did it seem like the bartenders kept disappearing and reappearing to you? Or was that just me?"

"Caught that too," Marianne said back. She held her drink in one hand tapping her short, French-tipped fingernails against the glass with her other, but she wasn't drinking any of the super expensive soda yet either.

Marianne hadn't dressed up particularly for their spying excursion, but since she was a weaver, and she owned a boutique that made custom clothing, she was always impeccably dressed, even when dressing down. Tonight, she had on a pair of long, straight-leg black pants that fit her perfectly—of course—and a white silk blouse with extra long cuffs. The shirt hugged her snuggly but the buttons didn't bulged across her chest like they were about to split apart, another sign of perfect tailoring. She'd been wearing a muted pink lipstick earlier in the day but dressed it up to a bright red for their mission, and even in the swirling lights, that red looked excellent against her dark skin. Her shortly cropped hair and the tiny winking diamond studs in her ears capped off a look of casual elegance Cary deeply admired.

"You think the appearing and disappearing thing is just a trick of the light?" Cary asked.

"Maybe." Marianne tapped her glass with her fingernails again. "Or maybe not."

Cary frowned at the crowd around them. She couldn't put her finger on what was weird about the place either. But her teeth were still on edge and the music was too loud and it was way too hot in here and a part of her felt the need to run away.

Fast.

But…why?

"What time is it?" Cary asked Marianne near her ear, even as she continued to scowl at the throngs of dancing people. The low vibrations of the techno music's base beat made her want to stomp out the tingles running up her legs.

"Eleven thirty," Marianne said. "Why?"

"Cause I'm getting antsier. And this place feels weird. And I'm thinking midnight is a thing in our world."

Actually, it wasn't always. Midnight wasn't the "witching hour" for a lot of supernatural beings. That was mostly human myth. In fact, in the nightclub world midnight was early. But she could practically feel time moving, in her bones, like a clock ticking down. And that made her wonder if there really was a clock ticking down.

And since it was coming up to midnight…

Well, maybe she was making things up. Just because the world contained spooky things most humans didn't know about, didn't mean everything *was* spooky and otherworldly. She just defaulted to that because of her job.

Still. The sense of dread in her gut built with the music and heat, churning through her blood with a rush of adrenaline.

Something was not quite right in this nightclub. She had no idea what that "not right" was, but there was definitely something more here than ordinary, mundane humans dancing the night away to a never-ending techno song, sipping on over-the-top expensive drinks.

And whatever it was, it was sending her Protector instincts into overdrive.

After hovering at the bar for another ten minutes, not drinking their sodas despite the heat and thirst, Cary and Marianne ventured out into the crowd again. The push and shove of bouncing bodies to a beat that hadn't seemed to change at all was even more irritating as they moved away from the bar. In fact, Cary's nerves were so wound up she could practically feel her skin crawling with the annoyance. Like bugs moving over her body.

The thought made her shiver. She looked back at Marianne, who was glaring at the crowds of people. "You okay?" Cary shouted, making sure her mouth formed the words clearly so even if Marianne couldn't hear her, she could read her lips.

"No!" Marianne shouted back. She motioned toward the back of the giant room.

Through the crowds, Cary spotted a bathroom sign, so she edged in that direction. Something about the music was officially grating against her nerves now, too. Not just the heat, which was humid and oppressive and gross, but the sound of that constant techno beat that just went on and on and on.

Geez, how was this place popular? Everything about it seemed perfectly arranged to irritate and cause grumpiness.

Her grumpiness, already surfaced after having to wait in an hour-long line to get in, was rising with each passing base beat.

And the lights. The swirling blues and reds and yellows that turned everyone into a hallucinogenic color-washed version of themselves. Yet another irritant.

Cary frowned at that. Most clubs were all swirling lights and heat and music. Yes, not usually the relentlessly unchanging beat this one seemed to have adopted. And not usually *this* tropical-jungle-hot. And maybe the lights chilled out once in a while in other places. Still, most of this was perfectly normal for a nightclub.

Wasn't it? Why was she so…annoyed?

Near the bathroom, the crowds thinned enough she and Marianne could stand against the wall without getting bumped around. She was desperately thirsty, but the soda in her hand was warm now, and the thought of drinking it made her stomach roll. Weird reaction, though. Any liquid should have satisfied. She noticed Marianne still hadn't drunk any of her soda either.

"Okay," she said, "so. I get why you think this place is… off. It is. I'm so irritable and grumpy right now I want to rip someone's head off. That's upper-level grumpiness, even for me."

Marianne smiled at that. "You're not grumpy most of the time. You just pretend to be."

"Ha! Anyway, my nerves are jumping, and I'm thirsty as all hell, but I'm not drinking this drink in my hand, and even the thought of drinking it makes my whole body rebel. That's not even a little normal."

"Same. And agree. Got any idea what's going on?"

"At a guess? Magic of some kind. But why the hell would you want to irritate people to make your club popular?"

"Maybe it's only irritating to us because your own Protector magic is keeping us from…whatever the magic is doing to everyone else." She gestured to all the bodies, all bouncing in rhythm to that relentless base beat. Hands in the air. Bodies and heads rhythmically jostling. Sweat dripping down the faces of those near enough for Cary to see. And everything a riot of colored lights.

If what was happening in this club was magic, and it was bad for those involved, Cary's magic would be working. It would be protecting her and Marianne from the magic right now.

"Is that why we're not drinking?" She looked down at her soda and her throat closed at the thought of getting it anywhere near her mouth. Wow. That was a big reaction to a glance at a warm soda. "Yup," she said, nodding at Marianne. "Must be something in the drink. How do you feel when you think about taking a sip?"

"Like I'm gonna throw up if I get this glass anywhere near my face," Marianne said.

"Yup."

"Drugs?"

"Possible. More likely magic, like a spell of some kind." She scowled. "Potion. That's the word. Potion. Wow, I'm annoyed. I can't remember words I'm so annoyed."

"We need to find out what's going on in here," Marianne said, looking at all the people on the dance floor. "Whatever's happening, it can't be good."

"If it was good, my magic wouldn't be working."

"Exactly. And I'm not sure all these people are doing well in the grips of…whatever is going on."

Cary looked even closer at the people nearest her. In her irritation, all she'd seen is sweat and dancing, but as she watched one woman in particular, she noticed the panic in her eyes, the tension furrowing her brow. She wasn't having fun, even though her body moved like she was deep into the party going on. Her mouth was pinched, not smiling and shouting at the music. A tear leaked over her cheek.

Oh, well, Cary couldn't have that.

She set her glass against the wall, near the baseboard, took Marianne's hand in one of hers and stalked up to the crying woman. She gripped her hand and tugged her close enough they bumped. Then she put the woman behind her.

It was a gesture, really. Symbolic more than practical. The trouble seemed to be all around them so putting the woman behind her made no difference to Cary's ability to protect her. Once inside Cary's shield, it didn't matter what direction the threat came from. And while Cary did tend to be in front of the people she protected, she could wrap them up in front of her and still keep them safe if that was necessary.

But the gesture signaled that Cary was officially protecting the woman now. At least to herself.

She backed everyone toward the bathrooms again. By the time they reached that small circle of breathing space, the woman was leaning hard against Cary's back and her sobs shook her entire body.

"Thank you, thank you, thank you, thank you…"

The litany poured out of the woman, the sound of her exhausted gratitude nearly breaking Cary's heart.

"I've got you now," she said. "You're safe." She glared at the dance floor, at all those people, some of them likely suffering like the woman behind her. She had to stop… whatever this was happening to them.

She faced the woman who sagged in her arms. "Can you talk?" she asked, hefting a little to keep the woman on her feet. A task which proved difficult at best.

Marianne took one side of the woman and together they eased her onto the floor near the bathroom door. Cary squatted down in front of her, keeping herself between the woman and the crowds, and finally got a good look at her.

She was a pretty woman with straight black hair decorated in glitter and sparkly hair clips. Her makeup had sweated off, leaving only a smudge of color on one cheek. Though her eyeliner and mascara still seemed to be intact, which was impressive as hell. Cary'd have to ask her what brand she used if they got the chance. The woman's round face was streaked with tears and sweat plastered her hair to her temples and neck. She was dressed for the club, in glittering black short shorts, a gold silk tank top, and four-inch mules. So Cary assumed she'd come here of her own free will.

Cary was certain she hadn't *stayed* of her own free will, though.

The woman gulped in a few deep breaths. "I can talk. I can talk. I think. But I couldn't stop dancing. I couldn't stop." She sagged against the wall. "So thirsty."

Cary glanced at the glass of soda she'd set against the wall. Marianne had set her drink down somewhere too. They exchanged a look but neither rushed to volunteer their untouched drinks to the woman.

"Let's start with names," Cary said. "I'm Cary. This is Marianne."

"Josie," the woman said.

"As in Josie and the Pussycats?" Marianne asked, her brows popping up.

"That was my mom's favorite show," Josie said with a faint smile.

"My sisters and I were named after my dad's favorite show growing up."

"You were?" Cary asked. Marianne had never told her that before. "Which one?"

"Gilligan's Island," Marianne said, shaking her head. "That show."

"Gilligan's Island?" Cary frowned.

"It's old. I'll make you watch it sometime." Marianne nodded back to Josie, and Cary shook off her distraction.

"Did you come here with others tonight, Josie?" Cary asked. She might have to wade into the mass of humanity to pull more people out.

Josie nodded. "Few of my girlfriends." She gestured to the dance floor. Her glittery nail polish sparkled in the swirling lights. "They're still in there somewhere. I lost track of them. We got separated." She pushed at the wall. "I need to go find them."

Cary stopped her with gentle hands on her shoulders. "You're too exhausted. I'll pull them out in a minute. First, tell me what was happening to you, if you can." When Josie frowned up at her, Cary said, "If you don't remember or want to talk about it, that's fine. Just tell me what your friends look like, and I'll go get them."

Actually, as she glanced at the crowd again, she realized what she really needed to do was shut this whole thing down. But how did she get between an entire crowd and…whatever it was making them dance to exhaustion, if she didn't know what that was? It had to be magic. A spell of some kind. Maybe if she shut off the music…?

"We heard this place was so much fun," Josie said, her voice quiet and faint beneath the base beat. "Everyone said it was *the* club. You know. The place you *had* to go. Even if that meant standing in line half the night."

"Yeah," Cary said, "uhm, who were 'they'?"

She was really curious how everyone was hearing about this place. She wouldn't have except that the club seemed to be taking customers from Gina's club. If Marianne hadn't brought the Haunt and Howl to her attention, Cary wouldn't have even noticed it was here.

Which was interesting.

She wasn't exactly a club bunny, out every night, going to the newest and latest. She worked too much, and when she wasn't working, she kind of liked quiet nights at home with her dogs, or a meal or movie night with the girls. Yes, they went dancing sometimes, and she loved that too. But not all the time. Frankly, her job was more than enough excitement for her most nights.

But that didn't mean she was completely out of touch with what was happening in her city's nightlife. She heard if a new club opened downtown, or there was a new fad sweeping the city. Eventually, information about that kind of thing popped up in her life somewhere.

The Haunt and Howl—according to Marianne—had been going strong for more than a month now. The kind of popular that ensured long lines and lots of attention. The kind of attention that meant she should have heard the name of the club mentioned…somewhere before this.

"I…" Josie frowned a little as she looked up at Cary. "I can't remember who I heard about this place from. I just remember thinking I *had* to come here. My friends and I…we were all really determined to get in, even if we had to wait for ages." She gave her whole body a shake. "I have to get my friends."

"I'll get them," Cary said. "Tell me what they look like."

"Why isn't this affecting you?" Josie asked. "Why aren't you…dancing?"

"Just a knack for these kinds of things." Cary waved the questions off with her usual non-answer.

She didn't tell people she was a Protector. For one thing, most people hadn't heard of them, which was for the best. Second, when she wasn't protecting people, she was an ordinary woman with no particular magic or skills or anything… She could barely do any of the self-defense moves her martial-arts-expert friend Lucy kept trying to teach her. She hadn't even known the supernatural world existed before getting tricked into her job. If she wasn't protecting someone, the magic she channeled but didn't control didn't work, leaving her vulnerable. So the fewer people who knew what she was, the safer she was.

Having the bad guys know she was vulnerable, and *when* she was vulnerable, would be bad.

"I think we need to stop all of this," Marianne said close to Cary's ear. "Not just get her friends out. I've been looking closer at all these people. They either look drugged out of their minds or terrified. There's no joy on that dance floor right now."

"Stop the music?" Cary asked.

"Might help. Depends."

Yeah. Depended on what was making everyone dance against their will.

"Where?" Cary asked. She hadn't seen a DJ booth or anything over the crowds.

"Got me," Marianne said, scowling at the writhing bodies.

"Josie." Cary faced the woman again. "Any idea where the music is coming from? Is there a DJ, or…?"

"We didn't see one when we came in," Josie said.

"What did you do when you got inside?" Cary asked.

"It was so hot in here, the first thing we did was get a drink," Josie said, wiping a hand across her sweat soaked brow. The gestured pushed some streaks of wet hair back off her forehead.

"What kind of drinks did you order?"

"You think they were drugged?" Josie sat up a little straighter. "We were so careful. We didn't turn our backs on the drinks. We watched out for each other…"

Cary calmed her with a gentling gesture as she tried to stand again. "If your drink was drugged, then everyone in here had the same experience. There wasn't anything you could have done."

"We all got something different. I had a Cosmo. Elle got a gin and tonic. Mina had a glass of wine. Tonya got a beer… All different."

Cary exchanged a look with Marianne.

"What happened after that?" she asked Josie.

"We finished our drinks pretty quick. I was so thirsty. I don't even remember drinking the whole thing. And then the need to dance was just overwhelming. The music was pumping. We were excited. We headed out into the crowds laughing. And then…"

"Then?" Cary prompted.

"I don't know. I… It felt like I was in control of what I was doing at first. Having fun, enjoying the beat, but then… It was like, like I couldn't stop. I got tired. I wanted to cool off, maybe get another drink, but I couldn't stop moving. When I tried, it was like it hurt to stop. But it hurt to keep going. I don't know how to describe it. No matter how hard I tried, I couldn't stop dancing."

Yeah, that was magic, all right.

Something in the drinks. Something in the music. Cary wasn't positive, but she was betting on the drinks after Josie's story. They might not be able to stop this even if they did find a way to shut off the music.

Shit. How did she protect these people? She couldn't get between them and something they'd already ingested.

But she'd pulled Josie out, enabled her to stop dancing. There had to be a way.

She glanced at the throngs of people. Too many for her to pull out individually. That would take most of the night, and some of them might get sucked back into the music again when she was off pulling someone else out.

She had to find a way to protect all of them at once.

But how?

She glanced back toward the bar. She couldn't see it from her vantage. There'd been people all around it, but she couldn't remember if any of them were drinking or not. Everything had seemed to be moving.

Even the mirrored wall of drinks.

The weirdness of this place, the never-ending dance…

It kind of reminded her of a fairytale. One of the real ones. With blood and guts and people chopping off body parts and dancing until they died.

If this was something to do with Faery and faeries, she was going to be so pissed.

Her mentor, Jaxer, the being training her as a Protector, was a faery. Her bosses were Fae. If this place was something to do with the Fae, they should have known and sent her here ages ago, damn it.

All these people!

She took a deep breath and racked her memory. She hadn't heard about a lot of unexplained deaths recently. There hadn't been a lot of emaciated bodies turning up all around the city. That had to be good, right?

Whatever was happening here, at least it wasn't killing people.

Yet.

"Okay," Cary said, straightening. "We have to stop all of this because if Josie was dancing to exhaustion, others are too, against their will. I can't pull them out one at a time. So we have to stop this at the source."

"The music?" Marianne asked. "Or the bar?"

"Both."

"How?" This from Josie.

Cary waved a hand vaguely in the air. "I have no idea." She stood and reached down to give Josie a hand up. "You think you can walk? You'll be safer if you stick with us."

Josie's grip on Cary's hand was surprisingly strong. "I can walk if I have to."

"You want to take your shoes off?" Marianne nodded down at Josie's four-inch mules.

They were adorable shoes, opened toed with sparkles decorating the thick straps over the foot arch, and platforms so the actual foot angle wasn't so steep. The heels were thick and chunky so they'd be easy to walk on. For a high heel, they were practical for long periods of standing on your feet. More practical than stilettos at any rate. At least for Cary.

But they were still heels. And Josie had been dancing for a while.

"I don't want to walk around in my bare feet," Josie said. "I'll keep them on."

Marianne pulled her purse off her shoulder and reached inside—it was a rectangular bag, smaller than a loaf of bread, just of a size to fit a wallet, a cellphone, and a lipstick, but not much else. Except that this was one of Marianne's purses. The outer size never reflected the size of the interior.

She pulled out a pair of cute black ballet slipper flats, frowned down at Josie's feet, put the ballet slippers back, rummaged around some more, and pulled out another pair of flats, these a more solid slip-on in a dark color Cary couldn't pick out in the swirling club lights.

"These should be about your size," Marianne said, handing the shoes to Josie.

"How did these fit in that purse?" Josie asked, her eyes wide.

"It's bigger than it looks," Marianne said, with a shrug.

Cary pressed her lips together so she wouldn't chuckle at the understatement. Marianne's bags were *always* bigger than they looked.

Josie gripped Cary's shoulder to keep her balance as she slipped out of her mules and into the flats. The moment she had both new shoes on, she sighed and looked up at them with a smile.

"Much better," she murmured. "I usually love these heels, but…" She glanced at the dance floor and shivered.

"Stick with us," Cary said. "You'll be safe." She frowned out into the crowd. "Bar or try to find the music first?"

"Bar," Marianne said. "We know where it is."

Cary snorted, and taking Josie's hand to keep her solidly behind her, they moved back through the dancing throng.

With both Josie and Marianne behind her, Cary knew her shields were active and protecting and that meant all three of them were safe. Still the push and shove of all those dancers, knowing that at least some of them were still dancing involuntarily, was both grating and horrifying. She was tempted to just keep pulling every person she passed out of the dance and behind her. But that would slow her down. She needed to stop all of this, not just try to rescue a few individuals.

When they reached the bar, the same two bartenders were busy at points separated by the huge length of the counter. The fact that they looked busy serving drinks, but no one seemed to be doing anything but dancing struck Cary as… odd. She supposed they could be serving new people just let into the club. Like her and Marianne. But with all the writhing bodies around them, very few had drinks in their hands.

Cary glared at the mirrored wall of alcohol behind the bar, the way it seemed to be moving backward and expanding as she watched. Everything on those shelves had to be drugged, or…whatever was wrong with the drinks.

What would happen if she threw something and shattered it all?

Outside of being noisy, destructive, and likely to get her thrown out of the club…it might just cause enough ruckus to stop the music and end the endless dance for those dancing against their will.

Hmm.

Well, it was her job to protect people. And if she had to break some glass to do it…

She shouted to Marianne. "Got something really heavy in that purse? I need to break some things."

Marianne glanced at the shelves of bottles. "Good idea?

Dangerous idea? What if whatever's drugging people shouldn't be released into a pile of liquid poison?"

That was something to consider. "I'll just stand between the wreckage and everyone else. That should prevent the mess from causing anymore harm." That was how her powers worked.

She couldn't get between the dancers and whatever it was they'd already ingested. And she couldn't get between the dancers and the source of the music yet because she didn't know where that was coming from. She had to plant herself between the good guys and the bad guys to protect the good guys, and when the "bad guys" weren't obvious, that made her job a whole lot more complicated.

Spilled drinks and possible aerosols of poison, though, were obvious. She could set herself up to protect everyone from something like that.

Probably.

She considered the wall again. She could leave this and try to find the source of the music and shut it down. Even if it didn't stop the dancing, the monotonous beat would at least stop scrapping over her nerves like nails on a chalkboard. But that would take time, and the more time they took, the more exhausted the unwilling dancers were getting.

Josie touched her arm as she considered the wall of alcohol. "I need to find my friends. I know they're in trouble. Whatever you're going to do, please do it. I have to help them."

Well that was a plea Cary could relate to. Protecting her friends was her top priority. Hell, it was the reason she was here.

"Breaking the bar it is." She nodded and looked back at Marianne.

Marianne gave a little shrug. "Okay. I'll trust you. But you're staying between me and that wall."

"I would be mad at you if you didn't stay behind me." She opened her hand, palm up, and waited for Marianne to hand her something heavy.

She was not disappointed. From the depths of her too-small-to-hold-this-much purse, Marianne pulled out what looked to be a tool box. The box roughly the size of two extra-large shoe boxes—the wide ones, big enough for men's tennis shoes—stacked on top of each other. Made of a dark plastic, the metal clip on the outside snapped into place, holding the lid shut, and a thick plastic handle on top. It should never have fit into Marianne's purse.

"What is it?" Cary asked.

"How was that in your purse?" Josie squeaked at the same time.

"Sowing kit," Marianne said.

"My sowing kit is the size of my hand and has like three needles and two colors of thread in it," Cary said.

Also, she never used her sowing kit. Her mom had given it to her when she went to college so she could repair buttons and things. Cary had hauled that little kit through several moves and jobs and still never used it. The thread had probably rotted away by now.

Marianne shrugged. "Never know what you might need to repair."

Cary grinned. Then more seriously as she hefted the weight of the sowing kit—which was significant—and said, "This will probably not be salvageable after this. Even if we could get it back, it's going to be covered in glass and whatever is in those bottles." For all she knew, what was in those bottles might dissolve the heavy plastic case.

"It's my backup," Marianne said with a wave, "not my favorite. It can be replaced."

"If you're sure."

"You gonna toss that thing, or will I?"

Cary bounced the case in both hands. Which wasn't as easy as it sounded. The thing probably weighed fifteen pounds. What the hell did Marianne have in there?

She gave the mirrored backwall side-eye, hefted the sowing kit…

And threw it into the shelves of glass.

CHAPTER 4

ary was not the athletic type, and under normal circumstances, she threw exactly like you'd expect a non-athletic type to throw. Badly. She threw things badly. She had precisely the lack of skills that meant she could have, under normal circumstances, thrown the fifteen pound sowing kit at the glass shelves that were only about six or seven feet away, and missed them all together. It was entirely possible she could throw that big ass box and have it land with an ineffective thud on the floor behind the bar, doing absolutely no damage at all.

But at that moment, she was protecting people. And her Protector magic gave her the skills she needed when she needed them. Mostly, she didn't need to *do* anything. She just stood between bad guys and good guys and let the shield do all the work. But occasionally, she had to put in more of an effort.

And when she did, she could do a lot more than she was normally capable of.

In this case, that meant throwing a giant ass sowing kit six

181

or seven feet into a wall of glass bottles like she was a Major League pitcher.

Glass shattered in a cacophony of noise loud even over the techno beat music. In the swirling, colored club lights, the destruction was a riot of rainbow glass shards flying everywhere. Liquid spilled out onto the floor, the mirror behind the shelves cracked and flaked off the wall.

Marianne and Josie both ducked instinctively. Cary raised her arm to keep glass from her face, though nothing actually got near her. When she was in full Protector mode, nothing harmful got through. And while she might have taken a non-lethal nick from some flying glass if it was ordinary glass, those bottles had held something that wasn't harmless. Which meant the glass had that dangerous stuff on it. Which meant Cary didn't have to worry about even tiny nicks or cuts.

On the other hand, the puddle of liquid that seemed to be growing disproportionately large under the shattered wall was a little worrying.

It wasn't melting the floor under it—she'd been a little worried about that—but it was glowing in a way that had nothing to do with the swirling lights. Glowing a purplish green color like a bruise. And sparkling. The sparkles were…interesting.

"Why is it glowing?" Josie asked, sounding horrified.

"And sparkling?" Marianne asked, sounding only slightly less horrified.

"Magic," Cary said with a shrug. She had no idea what *kind* of magic. She was still studying. But the sparkle and glow were a pretty big tell.

The liquid spread out behind the bar, growing like a little lake, taking over all the floor space. The two bartenders, who'd seemed oblivious to the destruction for a few moments, saw the liquid menace flowing toward them and both of them jumped up onto the top of the bar. Not just hopped up onto it butts first either. They leapt straight up and landed on their feet on top of the counter.

Not a human move.

Hmm.

The music didn't stop, but she noticed a few of the people closest to her stopped dancing to stare at the destruction. There was some head shaking, one man doubled over, his hands on his knees, and threw up. Ew. But also, huh? Exhaustion or the drink?

Or the smell.

The smell of all that spilled alcohol-magic ooze wasn't pleasant. Although it wasn't precisely *bad* either. Not like sewage or rot or anything. It was more like the sickly-sweet scent of rotting detritus in a jungle forest. Not in-your-face gross, but sort of subtly gross. The taste on her tongue was… something she'd have to rinse out later if she didn't want to keep tasting that stench all night.

As she was contemplating the stink, the two bartenders turned toward her. Almost as one. And headed in her direction, stomping across the wooden counter. She kept them in her peripheral vision but most of her attention was on the glowing liquid. It still seemed to be growing, which was bad since there weren't any more bottles shattering to feed the puddle. It was staying behind the bar and not leaking out, though, and that part was good. At least, she hoped it was.

The bartenders reached for her in unison, like bouncers ready to heft a troublesome patron out of the bar. They came up against her shield in unison too, stopped in mid-motion by the invisible barrier.

Josie gasped and stepped closer behind Cary.

Cary reached back to pat her arm. "Don't worry, you're safe."

The bartenders growled, the woman on Cary's right slapping at the invisible shield, the man on her left tried to hammer his fists into it. That just got him knocked backward a few steps and he wobbled, nearly falling into the liquid. He swung his arms wildly and pulled himself away from disaster, straightening with a glare at her.

"Don't want to touch the mess either?" Cry shouted at him. "Yeah, it doesn't look very pleasant. What the hell is it?"

"What have you done?" the woman on her other side shrieked.

"Just a little property destruction," Cary said. "What's the liquid goo?"

"You're dead now," the man growled. His voice was very low and the growl wasn't entirely human sounding.

Huh. "Shifter?" she asked aloud, not expecting an answer. It was possible. She wasn't sure what *kind* of shifter, but he was big enough and the noise he made could have been a shifter's growl right before shifting. But...most shifters didn't have magic or deal much with magic. Shape-shifting was biological, not magical. Just part of their physiological makeup. The magic all over the floor seemed to indicate something non-shifter related.

Though she was rethinking her Fae suspicions from earlier because this warehouse of a nightclub was filled with exposed metal beams. Lots and lots of steel everywhere. Steel was an iron alloy. And the Fae all, to some degree or other, had an allergy to iron. They weren't likely to spend time inside a nightclub constructed with exactly the kinds of stuff that made them break out in hives, or if the allergy was really bad, could kill them.

Her mentor Jaxer could manage most of the human world without too much trouble. His allergy was mild and he'd spent enough time in human cities to develop a resistance to iron. He could lean on wrought iron without breaking out in hives, and he could be inside her house without going into anaphylactic shock. He avoided getting into cars, and she was pretty sure wherever he lived, it wasn't inside a traditional house like hers, but otherwise, he managed pretty well in the city. Her Fae bosses were the same. They came and went from her house without issue. And she'd seen them materialize in places that would have sent other Fae into fits from all the iron.

But most Fae wouldn't purposefully set themselves up in a steel case like the nightclub.

So what kind of magic was this? And why?

The two bartenders continued to kick and punch at her shield. She mostly ignored them. She was keeping Josie and Marianne protected from the club, so she was safe inside her shield too. But the music was still pounding behind her, and not everyone had stopped dancing.

In fact, most people hadn't. Of the few closest to her who had, the guy who'd thrown up was passed out on the floor near the bar, outside the ring of dancers, but the others around him had gone right back to dancing.

Damn. "Gotta stop the music, too, I guess," she muttered.

"No!" the woman bartender roared and threw herself so hard against Cary's shield she was thrown backward, landing with a breath-stealing thud on her back on the counter.

"So… Guess stopping the music would be bad for them," Cary said.

"Means it's good for us," Marianne said. "Where to?"

"Got me." She watched the two bartenders, waiting for one to break.

The man broke first. He launched into the air, in a leap that would have impressed the most agile of cat shifters, and landed on one of the overhead beams. Definitely not Fae, she thought. Then he jumped again, landing at the opposite side of the nightclub and disappearing into the crowd.

"Okay, so the music is that way," she said. "But also, there's all this liquid magic stuff here that I don't want to hurt anyone." She thought of the guy passed out a few feet away, entirely too close to the bar. "If the bartenders are avoiding it, it's bad."

"Looks bad," Marianne agreed, wrinkling her nose.

"So I have to get to the other side of the club, but I don't want to leave everyone unprotected from the ooze." If she moved away from her position between the ooze and the dancers, she risked letting it get out from behind the bar. If she didn't move, she wouldn't be able to turn off the music and stop the never-ending dance.

Shit. She couldn't be in two places at once. Which was a pain in the ass.

"Got an idea," Marianne said. She rummaged her in bag again, longer this time, seeming to dig deep enough half her arm disappeared—into a space half the size of a bread loaf.

"That purse is amazing," Josie said with an awed sigh.

Cary understood her feelings. She was always impressed with Marianne's purses.

After some more digging, Marianne pulled out a square of what looked like yellow felt. It wasn't a very large square of yellow felt, maybe one foot by one foot. But since it was something Marianne had, Cary doubted the size of it reflected its reality.

"What's it do?" she asked.

"It'll soak up the mess. Hopefully not...conflict with whatever the magic is." She scowled behind the bar. "Whatever that is. But at least it'll keep it from leaking out."

"That little square of felt will stop *all* that liquid?" Josie asked.

"Should do," Marianne said, her focus on the bar. "I think…" She took the felt in both hands and reached over the bar, ignoring the woman bartender still trying to reach them through Cary's shield, then gently dropped the square into the middle of the liquid.

The sound of a sponge soaking up water had never sounded so comically exaggerated. Or loud. Cary watched the felt turn into a cube almost like a giant sponge and the liquid flow into that cube like a river running toward a lake. The cube kept expanding as it soaked up more liquid, until it took up a significant area behind the bar.

"Uh, how big will that get?" she said to Marianne.

"Big as it needs to. But…we should probably move away from the bar."

The hardwood counter made a groaning noise. The fact that they could hear the wood straining and the sponge soaking up the dangerous liquid even over the music was a little terrifying.

Or maybe it was just the Protector magic dampening the music? Cary wasn't sure. Could be. Though the music still sounded gratingly loud to her.

"Let's go shut the music off," she said. "This beat is giving me a headache."

The woman bartender shouted at them to stop, but Cary ignored her and pushed back into the crowds, Marianne and Josie in her wake, heading in the direction the male bartender had gone in his leap through the rafters.

Whatever he and the other bartender were, they weren't Fae if they were swinging from steel beams. And the way they moved really said shifter to her. But she had no idea what kind. Neither of them had the glowing yellow eyes she tended to associate with shifters. That just meant they weren't losing control of their animals yet. Which, she supposed, was a good thing. They weren't vampires. Vampires would have gone claws out for her neck earlier when she broke all the glass.

But the endless dancing and exhaustion, that still felt very Fae to her.

What the hell was going on in this club?

They reached the opposite wall from the bar, only stopping once when Josie spotted one of her girlfriends. They paused so Cary could pull her out of the dancing crowd.

She was easily a head taller than Josie, but Josie still held up the exhausted woman when she was finally inside Cary's protection and free from whatever spell was making her endlessly dance. Cary stopped long enough to make sure Josie and Marianne could support the exhausted friend, and then they pushed forward again.

Cary had to shut the music off and help all these people. Josie's friend looked like she was about to pass out. Marianne and Josie were practically carrying her. There were more people in this crowd that exhausted. Maybe even some close to collapsing.

What happened when they'd danced so far past their tolerance they did collapse? Where they even allowed to?

She was still pretty sure the dance hadn't killed anyone yet, but she wasn't absolutely certain it wouldn't. And that pushed her harder to end all this.

The wall opposite the bar just looked like a solid brick wall. The rest of the warehouse-sized nightclub had walls painted dark gray and washed with the swirling, colored lights. But this wall was brick and solid, and if it weren't for the nefarious dance going on behind her, Cary might have liked the aesthetic contrast between the brick and the gray walls. She looked around for the male bartender but didn't see him anywhere.

She also didn't see the source of the music.

It had to be here somewhere, damn it.

"Where the hell is the music coming from?" Marianne said, glaring at the solid wall.

"Good question," Cary muttered. She started feeling along the bricks, looking for…something. A hidden panel. Maybe an illusion. There had to be something here somewhere.

"Look!" Josie shouted.

Cary followed her pointed finger and realized there was a window in the brick wall, about six feet over her head. The glass was darkly tinted, almost black, so she couldn't see inside, even when she stepped back enough to get a better look. No light leaked out either. But that was the only thing in the brick wall that looked remotely like it might be the source of the music or the place the bartender had gone.

She studied the rest of the wall, looking for a door. A staircase. There had to be a way up there somehow.

Though, after seeing the way the man had jumped up to the ceiling beams without issue, it was possible he'd just leapt up to the window.

Which she couldn't do. Well, she might be able to if absolutely necessary. Her powers did let her move pretty fast when she needed to—not quite shifter fast, but still pretty fast. But she'd never had to jump a vertical that was so far outside her normal physical limits.

"Don't suppose you have a ladder in your purse?" she asked Marianne, staring at the window.

"Shouldn't there be stairs or something?" Josie echoed Cary's thoughts.

"If you spot them, let me know," she said to Josie, since Josie had had the eagle-eyes to see the window in the first place.

"I don't have a ladder," Marianne said. "But I do have some string in here somewhere."

"String?" Josie said.

Cary noticed she didn't deny the potential helpfulness of string. Josie seemed to be picking up on the more magical elements of the things that came out of Marianne's purse. She sounded more…curious than skeptical now.

Marianne rummaged in her purse again as Cary stared up at the window, hoping for a sign that that was where they had to go. Behind her, the continued thumping of so many legs moving on the wooden floor was a constant reminder that she had a whole club full of people to save and time was not on their side.

"What's happening?" Josie's friend said, her voice raw and rough over the music.

"Long story," Cary said, "but we're hoping to shut down whatever is making you all dance without stopping."

"It was horrible," Josie's friend said, though she was hard to hear over the music.

Cary heard Josie saying something to her friend, but they spoke too quietly now.

Marianne tapped her shoulder and she looked away from the window.

"This should help." She handed Cary a spool of thread.

It wasn't the small spools Cary had in her never-used sowing kit. It was a larger spool, a couple inches long and as thick as her wrist. The kind of spool Marianne used on the big sowing machines at her store. The thread seemed to be white, or some other pale color, but it picked up the multicolored lights flashing overhead so it was hard to tell its exact shade. There was a lot of thread on the spool. But it was thin thread. The kind for sowing up cloth. Not for climbing.

"What do I do with this?" she asked.

"Zig zag it on the bricks. It'll stick and give you a foot and finger hold to climb up."

Cary raised her brows. She trusted Marianne and Marianne's magical thread. She did not, however, trust her own rock climbing skills—which were non-existent. She frowned up at the window. It wasn't *that* high up. Even if she fell, she probably wouldn't break anything.

Maybe.

She took a deep breath, pulled out the end of the string and stuck it unceremoniously to the wall. It remained in place without any help at all. Cary ran the spool in a short, curving, switchback pattern, pressing the string against the bricks, and the string stayed in place. When she had it high enough she could no longer reach farther, she attempted to grip one of the "rungs" she'd just created.

And to her awe, she was able to hold the string and pull herself up, just like it was a thick ladder rung.

"Okay, you're officially the coolest person I know," Cary said to Marianne.

Marianne chuckled. "I've met some of the people you know, so I will take that compliment."

Cary glanced up at the window again. "I need you to climb up with me. I still need someone to protect or I won't be able to…do much." She leaned down to say this as close to

Marianne as possible so the other two women wouldn't overhear. She gave them a little nod. "But I'm not sure they'll be able to make the climb."

Josie's friend was leaning heavily against the brick wall, her head tipped back and her eyes closed. Josie was standing, mostly, but she had one hand on the wall propping herself up.

Marianne frowned at the two women, then at the dance floor. "I'm not sure I have anything in my purse that will block the magic. I didn't think to pack earplugs."

Since earplugs were so ordinary and Marianne's purse was filled with so much that wasn't ordinary, the fact that she looked annoyed by the oversight amazed Cary.

"I'm not sure I'll still be protecting them once I get to the window," Cary said. "The music is going to catch them again."

"Then we'd better move fast," Marianne said. "The quicker we stop that music and end whatever the hell is going on here, the better everyone will be." She settled her purse strap over her shoulder and motioned Cary up the string ladder. "I'll be right behind you."

Cary heaved in a breath and pulled herself up the ladder. When she reached the point where she'd left off sticking the string to the wall, she resumed pressing the switchback pattern into the bricks and climbed as she made the ladder. The fact that her toes stepped onto the tiny string and held as if it was a thick aluminum ladder rung awed her, but she kept her attention on building the ladder and not getting distracted by how cool the magic was.

They reached the window in a few minutes and Cary poked her head over the sill to see inside. The tint was too dark to see much, but there were shadowy movements inside, so there was definitely something in there beyond a storage room. She pressed at the glass.

And to her utter surprise, it swung inward on a hinge at one side of the window. The give was so sudden, she nearly lost her grip on the ladder and had to hold the now open sill to keep from falling backward onto Marianne.

"That was easy," Marianne shouted up at her.

"Uh huh." Maybe too easy. But one less complication was fine by her.

She hefted herself over the window sill and tumbled gracelessly into the room beyond, landing on the floor in a heap.

These were the awkward moments when she felt a lot less like a superhero and a lot more like she was in over her head in this job.

She glared back at the open window as it her awkwardness was its fault, and pushed to her feet. Then she gave Marianne a hand so she could—much more gracefully—climb inside the room too.

Once they were inside, Cary finally looked around.

In time to see the male bartender charging her.

She froze in place, watching him fly at her all anger and thick, muscled size. Her freeze instincts were, under ordinary human circumstances, probably not the best.

But they were perfect instincts for a Protector.

The man slammed against her shield and was flung backward onto his ass, halfway across the room.

Into the middle of what looked like sound tables inside a recording studio. Three large tables with knobs and switches and things all over them formed a U-shaped console. A single light right over the center of the console was the only light in the room so most of the space was dark and shadowed. None of the swirling, colored lights from the main floor here.

In the center of the console someone sat with their back to

Cary as they moved their fingers over the knobs and levers and switches on the panels in front of them.

"Okay." She had no idea what modern DJ equipment looked like, but this wasn't what she'd been expecting, to be honest. Though she wasn't sure what she'd been expecting.

To one side of the console, sat a shelf with dark green glass bottles stacked several deep. The bottles were roughly the size of a whiskey bottle, but squared instead of cylindrical, and the glass was textured with an abstract pattern of bubbles. At least, Cary thought the pattern was abstract. It was too dark inside the room and the glass was too deep a green to really see.

On the other side of the console, a smaller shelf contained three of those same green glass bottles with rubber tubes running into the bottles from the console. The tubes pulsed as something moved through them. And the green glass seemed to be glowing with whatever was being pumped into them.

Well, she had no idea *what* they were pumping into those bottles, but she knew whatever it was had to do with the never-ending dance and therefore it was the thing she needed to stop.

What would be better? Breaking the console or breaking the bottles?

She considered the bartender as he launched at her again. And finally, she saw that tell-tale yellow glow in his eyes. Shifter eyes.

One question answered. "What species?" she asked him when he crouched and glared up at her.

"What?" His voice was so deep now it made her bones vibrate.

"What kind of shifter? I'm still learning and my bosses would want me to ask."

He blinked. The yellow in his eyes flared. "Who the fuck are you?"

She waved a hand. "Just a concerned citizen. Here to stop…well, whatever it is you're doing since it's hurting the people below."

"You aren't stopping anything," the man growled and threw himself at her again.

"You keep doing that and not getting anywhere with it," she pointed out the obvious as he ended up on his ass again. "Maybe stop? Just a suggestion."

Keeping Marianne behind her, she headed toward the console and the glass bottles. The person in the chair at the console didn't turn around to face her. Which Cary thought was a little weird. She looked closer. They had a set of big, thick headphones over their ears. Short, straight blond hair under the headphones. And their hands on the console knobs were long-fingered and pale. But that was all Cary could see around their swivel chair.

The shifter—whatever species he was—kept leaping at her, even leapt up in the air and tried to land on top of her. That would have been terrifying if she wasn't protecting someone. The move got him flung to the wall under the window. And the bricks crunched when he hit them.

Oh boy.

She hurried to the glass bottles and reached to pick one up.

The minute she did, the person at the console swiveled around to stare at her.

"Don't touch those!"

Now that she got a better look, she wasn't any more sure who the person was. Or what they were. They were dressed in simple white t-shirt and white pants. Their eyes were pale pale blue. And their skin was that sort of white that was almost translucent. Their features were sharp and straight. A long face, with a pointed chin and straight, sharp nose. Blond brows were lowered over those pale eyes.

The person snarled at her. "Keep away," they said. "Touch those and die."

"Wow." Cary raised her hands in a calming gestured. "That's some threat for a few glass bottles. What's in them?"

"None of your business. Leave them alone."

"Gonna stop the music?" she asked. "Cause those people down there need to stop dancing."

"No."

Cary picked up one of the bottles. The headphones wearer nearly came out of their chair. The fact that they hadn't risen yet was interesting. But they pressed their hands into the armrests as if they intended on getting up.

Cary dangled the bottle in her fingers, holding it by the long neck but letting it wobble as if she didn't have a good hold on it. "What happens when I break one of these?" she asked.

From one side, the shifter launched at her again. She ignored him, holding the pale gaze of the person snarling at her from behind the console.

"I don't have another one of my handy magic sponges, by the way," Marianne said.

"Thanks for the warning." Cary twirled the bottle in the air. "What's in here anyway? For that matter, what was in the drink bottles? And what is all this about?"

The pale-eyed person just snarled harder.

"Those aren't answers. I hate when they don't answer questions." This to Marianne. "If they answered questions, I might not feel the need to experiment. Like, say, by dropping this glass bottle and watching it shatter and seeing what happens."

"Don't! You have no idea what you're doing," the pale-eyed snarler said.

"That's true," she replied cheerfully. "No idea. So maybe… I don't know. Explain it to me?"

"This is none of your business, human," the snarler snarled.

She grinned. "Well, I'm sure now you're not a human, so that's helpful. Thanks for that. What are you?" She raised a hand before he could answer and said, "I know that's a rude question, but I'm still studying. My mentor would be disappointed in me if I didn't ask."

"Still none of your business," the snarler said.

"Fair enough. I had to ask." She contemplated the bottle. "But without explanation, and knowing those people down there need to be freed from whatever the hell this game is, I'm gonna just have to go with total destruction."

The snarler screamed something at her, in a new-to-her language, but she'd already heaved the green glass bottle…

Right into the console.

CHAPTER 6

Glass shattered everywhere, chunks of thick green and bubbled glass imbedding in the console as sparks flew and crackled. Cary pressed her lips together. She'd never purposefully broken what was probably expensive electronic equipment before. There were a lot of firsts happening tonight.

Instead of the liquid she'd been expecting to explode from the glass bottle, though, a sort of steam or mist rolled out. It smelled strongly like sweat, which was distinctly unpleasant. And she'd swear she heard moaning in that mist.

Moaning? Like ghosts?

She shivered hard. She hated ghosts. Hated them to the depths of her soul. She was absolutely, down to her toes, terrified of ghosts.

"These bottles don't have ghosts in them. Do they?" She swallowed hard.

Marianne placed a reassuring hand on her shoulder. She knew how much Cary hated ghosts.

"What have you done?" the snarler roared.

The sparks and crackles of electricity drove them away

from the console, their hands in front of their face as the lights of short-circuiting electronics gave the previously dark room its own personal sort of strobe light effect. The scent of sizzling ozone mingled unpleasantly with the sweat stench from the broken bottle.

Cary contemplated another one of those bottles. She almost didn't want to touch one if it had a ghost in it. Could ghosts even be captured in glass bottles? Was that what was happening to people who died dancing? Gross. She hoped not. Still, there'd have been bodies left over if this many people had been killed and their ghosts captured. And as far as she knew, there hadn't been a huge upsurge in either missing people or dead bodies showing up around the city.

She looked back at the console, still sparking with blue and white light, the pale-eyed person attempting to get near the machine without getting hit by the strings of electricity arcing out. The green glass bottles attached to the console via rubber tubes had been glowing and the tube had been moving, which meant whatever was in the bottles was coming from the console.

Not ghosts then.

Probably.

But something. Something got pulled through the console, from the dancers, and put into the bottles. And whatever that something was, it smelled like sweat and it moaned when set free.

She shivered again.

"I think I should break another bottle and see what happens," she said.

"You sure?" Marianne nodded to the arcing electricity now snapping out at the pale-eyed person and forcing them back a few feet from the console. "Think you might have done enough damage."

"Wonder if that's stopped the music?" She couldn't hear the music anymore, but the two bad guys in the room were doing a lot of yelling and cursing, and the console was making a lot of angry damaged-machine noises, so that could be why.

"Hard to tell," Marianne said. "Want to head out and see?"

The console was looking a bit…explodey. She didn't particularly want to stand here while it exploded. But if she didn't, someone might get hurt. She needed a better angle to keep the people on the dance floor safe though.

But as she started toward the window, the woman bartender leapt into it, blocking it fully, her growl loud in the already chaotic cursing.

"Definitely shifters," Cary murmured. "Any idea what they are?" Since they hadn't seen fit to tell her. Marianne had been a weaver her whole life, which meant she'd been aware of the preternatural world a lot longer than Cary. She might have encountered…whatever kind of shifters these were at some stage.

"No idea," Marianne said with a shrug. "Something big, though. Bear, maybe?"

"Are the human forms of all bear shifters big?" she asked. She'd have to look that up. The human form of a shifter didn't necessarily translate to the size of their animal form. But maybe bear shifters were larger in their human form if they shifted to big bears?

The console gave a loud cracking noise and the plastic casing started to pop and heave.

"That's not good," she said.

The shifter woman in the window looked at Cary and her now glowing yellow eyes narrowed. "What did you do?"

"Broke some more bottles," Cary said. "Want me to get

between you and the explosion so you don't get hurt?" She hated protecting bad guys. But her job was to protect people and sometimes even the bad guys needed protecting. Didn't mean she had to like it when that happened, though.

The woman looked at the console. "Fuck this," she said. "They haven't paid us enough to get blown up."

"Who's they?" Cary asked, but the woman had already disappeared back through the window.

"Good hint, though," Marianne said. "Hired thugs."

"Yup. Wonder who hired them." And she wondered if the pale-eyed snarler who was not human was one of "them" or just more hired help.

The male shifter, who'd stopped launching attacks at her to try and help the pale-eyed snarler with the console, looked between the console, the open window, and the console again. "She's right. No pays worth this."

"Come back!" the pale-eyed snarler shouted, but too late. The man had leapt back through the window, following his fellow bartender.

Cary sighed. "Guess I'll never know what kind of shifters they were now."

Marianne patted her shoulder. "Sometimes we don't get the answers."

"I know. It's just frustrating. I hate not knowing. Plus, I'll have to hear about it from Jaxer." Who, she thought, should already have known about this place and sent her here weeks ago, so maybe she could avoid a lecture by lecturing him first. Yeah. That sounded like a plan.

"You've ruined everything!" the pale-eyed being said. "They'll kill us now. Do you understand? They'll kill us."

Cary sighed. "Who. Is. They?"

She shot a look at the console as it cracked some more and internal wires and electronic guts popped out, sparking off more electricity. Wow, that was a lot of destruction from one glass bottle full of mist. Or whatever it had been. Not a ghost. It definitely hadn't been a ghost.

"Listen," she said, "that machine of yours is about to explode. Let me just get between you and it, so no one gets hurt, and then you can explain everything so I don't go home irritated."

She started toward the pale-eyed being, but they snarled at her—because of course they did—and lunged in her direction.

She shifted her stance, to protect Marianne and face the attack, but the pale-eyed snarler didn't reach for her. Instead, they grabbed at the green bottles, scooping up seven or eight into their arms.

"Uh...? Not sure that's helping anything." But the snarler's frantic efforts did enable her to get between them and the console, so no one got blown up.

Because it looked more and more like that console was about to explode. The crackling was louder. The arcs of blue-white electricity snapped up to the ceiling now. The sizzling sparks jumped around the room. The bottles that had still been attached to the console shattered and released more moans.

Cary held very still as that sound went through her and made the hairs on her neck rise. Ugh. Not ghosts, she told herself. Not ghosts. But *boy* did whatever it was sound like a ghost.

The snarler managed to get about ten glass bottles into their arms before giving the lost console another frantic look. "You've ruined everything," they shouted at Cary. "They'll kill you too."

"No," she said. "But it would be very very helpful if you'd tell me who 'they' are."

"*They* are ancient. And they need this energy. *They* are vindictive. And they will destroy the human who got in their way."

"*That* still doesn't tell me who *they* are," Cary pointed out.

"Your doom," the snarler said.

Cary sighed. "Now, how often have I heard that? My doom. How ridiculous. Just give them a name or don't." She huffed. "My doom."

"Gotta be Fae," Marianne said. "People only ever talk about the Fae that way."

"Oh, I don't know, I've heard vampires talk that way about the Master of Portland before. All awe and threat." She hadn't personally met the vampire Master of Portland yet. Ariel was rumored to be pretty terrifying, so she didn't particularly want to meet her either. "But this doesn't seem like a vampire scam. Be more blood involved if it was vampires, right?"

"Probably," Marianne agreed. "I'd put money on Fae."

"Fae working with shifters and... What are you?" she asked the pale-eyed person again. Probably not Fae with all the electronics around—too much iron in the metal parts of the equipment. But someone who worked for Fae? Or a Fae, but one without a strong iron allergy, like Jaxer? That was possible, she supposed. Hell, for all she knew the pale-eyed person was a wizard or sorcerer or something. There were a lot of magical beings in the world.

So much still to learn. She sighed.

The console cracked and hissed and sparked and the noise of it all got suddenly louder. "Oh oh," Cary muttered. She edged toward the window, keeping Marianne behind her. "Better get over here," she said to the pale-eyed being, whatever they were. "Quick." She waved them toward her.

Instead, the person grabbed one last bottle and lunged to one side of the room… To a door Cary hadn't seen earlier just beside the bottle filled shelf.

They disappeared through before Cary could so much as shout.

And then the console exploded.

ary turned her head to one side and put a hand up to cover her eyes from the blinding white light filling the room. The explosion of plastic and knobs and wires and glass died as quickly as it happened. Leaving the room eerily silent in its wake.

She blinked away the spots in her eyes and glanced over her shoulder at Marianne. "Okay?"

"Fine. Thanks for blocking that." She waved at the melted chunks of the console scattered all around the room.

More of the glass bottles had shattered in the explosion, leaving the floor glittering with sharp green shards in between twisted hunks of plastic and frayed wiring.

"What a mess," Cary said, wrinkling her nose. Now the room smelled like sweat and burnt plastic. "Still like to know what they were capturing in those bottles, though."

"At a guess," Marianne said, "the energy from the dancers. There are a few Fae who live off the energy of other beings. The pale one with the headphones said they needed the energy, whoever *they* were."

"Why did the energy *moan* when it was released?"

Marianne shrugged. "Unhappy people forced to dance until they're exhausted while this…" She gestured at the remains of the console. "While this collects all their energy? I'd moan from the exhaustion, too."

"Fair enough. Still." She shivered. Too much like ghosts for her liking. "Shall we check on the crowd below?"

The music had definitely stopped behind them in the main part of the club. Replaced by the sounds of a lot of people talking at once.

"Don't want to go after the bad guy?" Marianne asked, nodding to the door.

"What am I going to do if I catch up to them? Not like I can arrest them for collecting energy to feed a mysterious *they*."

One of the big problems with her purely defensive job. She could keep good guys safe from now to the end times, but she couldn't actually *do* anything about the bad guys. She could stop them doing bad things in the moment, but she didn't have any offensive tricks up her sleeve to keep them from doing bad things in the future. She was a walking, talking Kevlar vest. And Kevlar vests had their limits.

But at least for tonight, they'd stopped…whatever the hell had been going on in this club.

"I think we've ruined the club, too." She nodded at the console wreckage. "So I don't think Gina has to worry about this place being competition anymore."

"She'll be glad of that." Marianne shook her head. "Can't tell her why the place failed, though."

"The authorities will come up with some reasonable explanation," Cary said.

They always did. Things that sounded logical. Better that way. Kept humans in the dark about the otherworldly things living next to them. And that was better for everyone involved.

"Bad wiring," Marianne said with a nod.

"Didn't meet code," Cary said.

"Dangerous negligence."

"There you go. All sorted."

They climbed back down Marianne's string ladder because Cary wasn't sure where the door went, and she wanted to check on Josie and her friends sooner rather than later.

By the time they hit the main floor, the cacophony of noisy people all talking at once was almost as loud as the music had been. The strobe lights had stopped strobing but were still on, so there were pools of color around the giant dance floor, washing people in one spot with blue and in other with yellow, still another group were lit by red.

Josie and her friend were hugging two other women to one side of the string ladder. When Josie spotted Cary and Marianne, she ran over and swept them up in a tight hug, too.

"Thank you, thank you," she said. "You stopped the music. Thank you so much."

"Everyone okay?" Cary gestured to the other three women.

"Fine. Exhausted enough to drop. But fine. Now." She glanced up at the open window. "What happened?"

Cary waved a hand. "Weird music table. Green bottles. Explosions. You know, no big deal."

Josie blinked at her. "I... I don't know how to respond to that."

"Don't worry about it." Cary grinned. "Just maybe don't come back to this club again."

"It'll probably close anyway," Marianne added. "Bad wiring."

"Didn't meet code," Cary said.

"Dangerous negligence," Marianne said.

Josie frowned. "Uh. Okay. What was in the drinks? It sparkled."

Cary had no idea still, but given this was probably something to do with the Fae—even at a distance—it was likely magic. "Probably some sort of hallucinogen," Cary said, going with a mundane answer Josie would understand. "Keep everyone dancing and drinking so they could keep making money."

"Dangerous negligence," Marianne said again.

"They will not survive the scandal," Cary said.

Josie glanced between the two of them. "I'm missing something, aren't I?"

"Nothing you need to worry about," Cary said. "Everyone's safe now. You and your friends should get home, though. It'll probably take a few days to recover from the exhaustion of all this."

Especially since some of their energy had been stolen by a magic music console.

Cary and Marianne made sure Josie and her friends left the club without issue and then followed them out, leaving the rest of the crowd to disperse on their own, most of them wandering off in dazed confusion.

In the cold, sharp air outside, Cary pulled in a deep, cleansing breath. The chill felt wonderful after the heat inside the club, and the air was fresh and smelled like approaching rain, which helped clear the stench of sweat and burnt plastic from Cary's nose.

"So, all that heat to keep them sweating to keep them drinking to keep them dancing?" she said to Marianne.

"Maybe just to get them to drink as soon as they got inside," Marianne said. "We nearly did."

"True enough." Cary glanced across the street and a shadow leaning against the window of a closed restaurant caught her attention. She scowled, checked traffic, and jogged across the street, Marianne keeping up with her without asking questions.

"Jaxer," she greeted her erstwhile faery mentor with a little frown, hands on her hips as she stared him down.

He was, as usual, ridiculously handsome—tall, blond hair, green-blue eyes, sharply chiseled features—and wearing ridiculously inappropriate-for-the-weather clothing—a cobalt blue silk shirt opened at the collar to show off his muscles and light, tan linen trousers that rippled in the cold wind.

Cary shivered just looking at him. "You need a jacket," she huffed.

He spread his hands. "And hide all this?"

She didn't rise to the tease. "Shut up. What are you doing here?"

He nodded to the club. "What are *you* doing here?"

"Helping a friend." She waved over her shoulder to indicate Marianne.

"Hi Marianne," Jaxer said with a sexy grin.

"Hi, yourself, handsome. Was this a Fae mess?"

Cary loved how Marianne didn't beat around the bush. That was one of the reasons they were best friends. Plus, Marianne wasn't impressed by Jaxer's charm. She lapped it up when she felt like it, but she wasn't impressed by it. Jaxer was frequently too charismatic for his own good, so it amused Cary when other people didn't fall victim to him. She couldn't at this stage because…well, she'd been working with Jaxer for long enough now that his ability to irritate and annoy her far outweighed his appeal.

"This was, indeed, a Fae mess," he said without prevaricating.

Which surprised the hell out of Cary. "You're admitting it? I expected some deflection."

He shrugged. "Not *my* Fae mess. No reason to deflect. Some of the old ones from Europe have been running this nightclub scam for a few years. Luring in humans, stealing their vitality. Old school type of Fae game. They'd hire whatever local members of the preternatural world could be hired to staff the place and then suck up all the energy while their hired help took all the money."

"They didn't want the money too?" Marianne asked.

"No need for it," he said. "Fae wealth is measured differently to human wealth."

"Ha," Marianne said. "Tell that to the goblin king."

Jaxer frowned a little, but Cary didn't want to get sidetracked onto the topic the goblin king's continued attempts to kidnap Marianne and make her weave gold for him.

"If you knew about this," she said, to get Jaxer back to the topic at hand, "*why* has this been allowed to go on for a full month here without you or the Nags sending me in to stop it?" This was just exactly the kind of job her bosses usually sent her out on. The fact that they hadn't was very suspicious.

"We've been trying to track down the Fae behind the whole scam. No one here in the US or in Europe has been able to find the specific Fae behind the clubs. And since it's going to get the attention of humans soon, the European Fae are actually cooperating with the North American Fae to try and find the culprits. We didn't send you here to stop them because we were working on dragging the big bosses out of the dark."

Cary winced. "And I messed that up."

He shrugged again, not looking particularly bothered by the fact. "I didn't agree with letting this place go for so long, so I can't say as I'm upset you…" He frowned a little. "What exactly did you do?"

"Blew up the console they were using to suck the essence from all the dancers by throwing a bottle of that essence at the console," she said.

"Huh." His lips twitched, like he wanted to smile. Or laugh. Or maybe scowl. It was a little hard to tell. "Worked?"

"Worked. Music stopped. All the bad guys got away, but the good guys are all safe and sound now."

"Then you did a good job, protégé. Well done you."

"Ha." But she preened a little at his praise.

"So now what?" Marianne asked. "These clubs keep popping up around the country and you all just let them go?"

"They won't pop up in Portland anymore," Jaxer said. "Pretty sure they'll attempt to stay as far away from Cary's destructive nature as possible now."

She scowled at him. He ignored her.

"But the rest… That's a Fae problem."

"Hmm." Marianne pressed her lips together. She didn't look any happier with his answer than Cary was.

"A Fae problem that will be taken care of so no more humans are hurt," she said to Jaxer, her chin lowered. "Right?"

"Right," he assured. When she continued to glare at him with her chin tucked, he raised his hands, palms facing her. "I swear. We will stop the scam. Sooner rather than later. And no more humans will be harmed. Fair enough?"

"Fine." She huffed out a breath. "But if I hear this shit is still happening, I'm going to have words for you and the other Fae."

His grin was quick and, unusually, real. "I would expect nothing less."

He flung an arm around her shoulders and then Marianne's, pulling them gently down the street. "Now. Shall I treat you both to a late dinner?"

"You better," Marianne said.

"With lots of undrugged drinks, please," Cary said, still super thirsty from the heat inside the club.

"And then I'm going home to give Gina the good news," Marianne said triumphantly. "The Haunt and Howl is no more."

Cary chuckled but glanced over her shoulder at the club.

A few remaining stragglers stumbled out the front door, blinking at the street, pulling their coats closer around them. The bouncer who'd been at the door had vanished completely and so had the line of customers waiting to get in. Even the ropes that had been on the sidewalk to keep the line orderly were gone. The giant brick building just looked like an abandoned warehouse now, with blacked out windows high up, and an unlit sign over the door.

Whatever authorities showed up to investigate this mess were going to have a lot of questions. Cary was just glad she didn't have to hang around and answer any of them.

She let Jaxer and Marianne pull her down the dark sidewalk, the soft glow of streetlamps lighting their way toward Chinatown and some good late night dinner options. She could hear the sirens in the distance. The farther they got from the club, now, the better.

But going forward, she was going to stick to nightclubs where she knew the owners.

Just in case.

THANK YOU

I hope you enjoyed this contemporary fantasy collection. Putting this book together has been a delight, and I very much enjoyed writing all five of these stories, exploring the fun to be had in the fantasy genre. Especially with so many different kinds of guardians.

For those who are new to Cary Redmond, the main series starts with the novel, The Trouble with Black Cats and Demons. There are also a number of short stories in the series, some of which have been assembled into their own collections. For the origin stories of Cary meeting most of the important people, and pets, in her life, start with When Cary Met the Good Guys.

You can also keep reading for an excerpt from The Trouble with Black Cats and Demons.

Thanks again for picking up Haunts and Howls and Guardian Spell!

EXCERPT

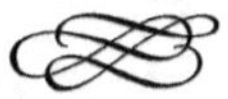

THE TROUBLE WITH BLACK CATS AND DEMONS

CHAPTER 1

"Not again." Cary Redmond ducked as another fireball clipped over her head. "You don't think fireballs are a bit over the top," she shouted up at the ceiling then had to duck again as a dagger whispered past her ear.

Close. Her heart pounded. Way too close.

She needed to find the damned cat and get out of here. She scanned the apartment from her dubious cover behind a table piled high with unopened mail. Fireballs, daggers, gusts of preternatural wind, freezing hail, and the occasional lightning bolt dropped around her, roaring through the living room in a bright cacophony of magical mayhem.

The lightning bolts flashing in the small confines were pretty spectacular. If they hadn't been trying to fry her, she might have enjoyed the show.

"Jaxer, I'm going to kill you for this."

Normally, this kind of thing was just a part of her job. She was a Protector and literally got paid to run around keeping people safe, mostly from magical bad guys. Not that she'd asked for the job, but that was another story. It *was* her job, so she faced off against dangerous stuff because the Nags—her bosses—told her to.

Tonight, however, was not an official assignment. Tonight, she was just doing a favor for her demented faery mentor. The bastard knew exactly how to get to her. All he had to do was mention a defenseless little black kitty cat and she was done for. How could she refuse to help a kitty? People did rotten things to black cats on Halloween.

Except Jaxer had forgotten to warn her about the fireballs.

She screeched through her teeth and dove behind the couch as one of the aforementioned fireballs barreled toward her. She cursed Jaxer as she took a quick look under the couch for the cat. Where the hell was it?

She'd called out to it when she'd first entered the apartment but hadn't gotten any irate kitty responses. After her lurching hunt of the living room and kitchen, the only place left was the bedroom.

She pulled in a deep breath as she contemplated the long space of unprotected ground between her hiding spot behind the couch and the bedroom door. Once she found the cat, this would be easier. When she was actively protecting something, very little of the magical dangers could get to her, and nothing deadly would touch her. She just had to *find* the cat first. And quickly. They had to be out of this cursed apartment before midnight. Before the wizard got home and all hell broke loose.

Again.

She ducked flying objects and ran to the bedroom, squealing when a lightning bolt hit the ground right behind her. Crossing her fingers that there were no nasty spells waiting for her, she lunged through the half-open door and cringed in anticipation of magical repercussions as she fell onto a red-carpeted floor. She held perfectly still, waiting.

Nothing. She let out a breath and pushed herself up onto her hands and knees, shaking her head. All this for a cat. That bastard Jaxer had a lot to answer for.

She rose to a crouch, trying to calm her racing pulse, and froze.

In front of her sat a huge bed, which she barely noticed because the naked man lying in the middle of the enormous mattress stopped her heart.

Holy shit.

He was absolutely magnificent. Tanned skin, well-defined muscles, thick, black hair hanging down over his forehead. He was lying against a giant headboard with his head hanging forward so she couldn't get a good look at his face, but his golden eyes seemed to glow up at her from under his brows. Piercing and stunning and breath-stealing.

Cary swallowed. Hard. Because even the captivating gold of his eyes wasn't enough to keep her gaze from wandering over the breadth of his naked chest, the corded muscles of his shoulders and arms, the flat expanse of his stomach. It took a great deal of will power not to follow the line of dark hair arrowing down his abdomen…lower.

The man straightened and Cary heard the clink of chains at the same time as she got a look at his neck—and the thick collar covering most of it.

What the hell had Jaxer gotten her into?

"Who're you?" she asked, breathless and embarrassed.

"Who are you?"

His voice carried a deep reverberation that made her spine tingle. Oh boy.

"I'm looking for a black cat," she said, knowing the explanation sounded inane. Jaxer had told her about Sheldon the Wizard, but this? This was something else all together. What was this guy doing here? He wasn't Sheldon, she was sure of it. But then who was he? And where was the cat?

She blinked and a black leopard lay on the bed where the man had been. She sucked in a sharp breath, blinked again. And the man was back.

"Whoa." Cary swallowed. "*You're* the black cat I came to rescue?"

Oh, she really was going to kill Jaxer now. He hadn't said anything about a fully grown man who happened to be a leopard shapeshifter. He'd made sure she thought she was after a little, harmless kitty cat, not a deadly dangerous big cat who shifted into a beautiful, naked, very large man.

The faery was dead. Not that she knew how to kill him, but that was beside the point.

"Jaxer sent you?" The man's eyes narrowed and his features took on a dangerous edge. He hissed a curse under his breath and shook his head. "Stupid."

"Hey!" She stood, the better to face his gorgeous disgust. No one should look that good while insulting you. "You could have done worse, buddy."

She took a step toward the bed, wiping damp palms on her jeans. The chains she'd heard earlier linked the collar on his neck to the headboard, which was brass and made-up of a scrawl of symbols she didn't recognize but looked like they might mean something if she stared at them long enough. He wasn't bound anywhere else that she dared peek, and the chains appeared flimsy enough. So obviously the power keeping him confined was in the collar.

"What is that?" She gestured with her head toward the thick band of metal.

"A binding ring," he said slowly, as if speaking to a child.

She frowned, both at his tone and the news. "But you just shifted."

"It's been designed to contain both my forms. Any other questions before you get me out of here?"

"Yeah, what crawled up your butt and put you in such a pissy mood?"

"Being held captive for sacrifice by a wizard and having a child sent to rescue me has dampened my day a bit," he said.

She grinned and enjoyed watching his eyes narrow suspiciously. "Child, huh? You know, at my age that's a compliment."

"How old could you be? Twenty?"

She shook her head. She'd actually turned thirty-one last April. But when she got tricked into becoming a Protector at twenty-five, she'd stopped aging at a normal rate. One of the few things about the job that didn't irritate her.

She took a quick moment to glance around the rest of the room. The red carpet wasn't the only gaudy element. Lots of black leather covered the walls and an animal skinned rug, which she was afraid to think about too closely given the captive on the overlarge bed, was tossed across the floor in front of what she thought might be a closet. A wood and metal trunk sat against one wall, red silk drapes covered the single window, and the overhead light was covered by thick, dark metal chains which gave the room strange shadows.

Fortunately, there were no nasty attack spells in here, which meant Sheldon the Wizard didn't want his captive accidentally hurt by a stray lightning bolt. That worked in her favor, giving her time to solve the binding ring problem without being pelted by hail.

Though even if there had been spells in here, now that she was officially protecting someone, she could keep them both safe.

She did wonder why Sheldon would care if his shape shifting captive got hurt before the midnight sacrifice.

Obviously, he didn't want him dead. You couldn't sacrifice something that was already dead. But an additional warning spell in here probably wouldn't have killed his prisoner. Maybe. If Sheldon had enough control.

If he didn't, and was as powerful as Jaxer claimed, they really needed to get out of here. Fast.

She eased up to the bedside, still leery of traps, and leaned in close to the leopard man, trying to ignore the yummy, stomach-fluttering male scent of him as she studied the binding ring. It was a thick band of silver and copper intertwined in a complex pattern of twists and turns. Over the silver, tiny runic symbols danced and shimmered so they were nearly impossible to read.

"Oh good," she said, "a hard one."

The prisoner shivered, a low growl rising from his throat. The sound made Cary's heartbeat jump.

Speaking of hard ones.

She could feel his glare on the side of her face, but she resisted looking. She had other things to worry about at the moment.

Like how the hell she was going to get this damned magical containment brace off his neck without alerting the entire mystical neighborhood.

"You did that on purpose," the man snarled.

"Huh?" She glanced at him. "What are you talking about?"

"Don't breathe on me again," he said.

She scowled. "What am I supposed to do? Hold my breath until I get your collar off? Just relax, big guy. You'll be out of here in a minute." To herself, she mumbled, "Wouldn't have gotten this much grief from a proper black cat."

"You some kind of witch?"

"No." After a moment, she sighed and shook her head.

"Well, there's no help for it. I'm gonna have to use brute force. It'll take too long to get this off subtly."

"We don't have much time. It's nearly midnight now."

"Gee, really?"

He ignored her sarcasm. "Brute force?"

"Hold onto your valuable body parts," she said and tried not to think about his exposed valuable parts. Then she wrapped her hands around the collar, easing her fingers gently under so the backs pressed against his neck. His skin was warm and another shiver danced down her spine.

"Wait."

She met his gaze.

"What the hell are you doing? If I can't break that with my bare hands, you can't—"

He stopped short when she tugged and the collar came away with a quiet click.

"I'm not without some talent," she murmured.

"Who *are* you?"

"Come on. We have to get you out of here. I just made a lot of magical noise with that little stunt."

"Hold on."

He grabbed her hand. The feel of his warm palm wrapped around her fingers sent tiny sparks of electricity dancing over her skin. He dropped his hold, but she saw his eyes widen with the same shock she felt. He inhaled deeply, and against her will, she watched the strong muscles of his chest rise and fall.

"What's your name?" he asked.

"Cary."

"Cary. I'm Deacon."

"Nice to meet you." Did that sounded as stupid to him as it did to her given the circumstances?

He smiled, a slow, deadly grin that made her pulse race. "Nice to meet you, too."

She blinked and shook her head. "Come on, Deacon. We need to move."

As he slid to the edge of the mattress, Cary turned her back to avoid embarrassing them both—despite the temptation to look over every inch of him. The sound of material moving over skin behind her didn't help curb her less polite impulses, though, so she hurried to the door to see how the lightning bolts and fireballs were doing.

Slipping into his jeans, Deacon watched the woman as she peeked around the edge of the doorframe at the living room and the still popping spells Sheldon had set to keep help from reaching him.

She wasn't the rescue he'd been expecting. He'd expected the damned faery to come himself.

Jaxer had convinced him to let the wizard "capture" him, so they could find out *why* Sheldon was kidnapping shifters. They'd only found a few of Sheldon's victims—their bodies anyway. And they'd been little more than desiccated husks. The rest of the missing shifters... Even their bodies had vanished.

Wizards didn't typically go after shapeshifters for sacrifice. They were too hard to contain, and most of them didn't have the kind of magical energy an average human wizard could absorb through ceremonial magic. Shapeshifting wasn't typically magic. It was just a species trait.

Deacon knew none of the shifters killed so far had had any actual magic. He was a different case, but he was pretty sure Sheldon didn't know that. Jaxer did, which was why he'd come to Deacon in the first place, and Deacon had felt obliged to help even though none of the shifters taken had been leopards.

He suppressed an irritated growl. This was the last time he'd let the faery use him for bait. He'd been chained to that fucking bed all day with no sign of help. Then Jaxer went and made things worse by sending in this…woman to rescue him instead of coming himself. How dare he endanger someone else when this crusade against Sheldon was his own personal business? Bad enough he dragged Deacon into it.

But as Deacon watched the woman straighten away from the doorframe when a lightning bolt flashed, he realized there *was* something about her. He couldn't deny the power she must have to break through the binding ring. Yet she looked and smelled like a normal, human woman.

Her light brown hair hung in long ponytail her back over a battered brown leather jacket. She wore jeans, hiking boots, and a purple t-shirt with a glittery Happy Halloween emblazoned over a maniacally grinning jack-o-lantern. Her blue eyes had sparkled when he'd called her a child, then flashed with irritation when he'd insulted her. And for reasons he couldn't quite understand, he'd found it hard to look away from her, especially when she'd knelt next to him on the bed.

Something about her…something about her scent tugged at his instincts.

Who the hell was she? *What* was she? She had to be more than human, but none of his sense picked up anything particularly preternatural about her. So where did all that power come from?

Jaxer had some serious explaining to do.

Deacon shook off his preoccupation and walked up behind her to stare at the living room over her head. Black scorch marks marred the hardwood floors, and a layer of frost covered one side table. The air was heavy with electricity and the smell of burning ozone.

Despite the multiple magical eruptions, the apartment was in remarkably good shape. As he watched, a dagger flew toward the bedroom, dropped harmlessly a foot from the doorway, and disappeared as if it hadn't existed.

Clever. Less clean up. And a testament to Sheldon's power.

He couldn't blame Jaxer for being worried about the little shit. But given a choice, Deacon would have taken a more… active approach to getting rid of the wizard.

Unfortunately, and he was reluctant to admit this even to himself, his approach probably would have gotten him killed. The bastard wizard was powerful. How Sheldon managed to be so powerful at his age was a mystery. But maybe that was the reason Jaxer was so obsessed with finding out the *whys* behind Sheldon's actions.

If Deacon got out of this apartment alive, he'd ask the faery. In the meantime, he and this very human woman in front of him had to navigate the bespelled living room and get away before Sheldon got back.

Deacon drew in a slow breath and was hit again by Cary's scent. Vanilla and cinnamon. And something else. Something that shot jolts of lust and need through his gut, making him lean closer to her just so he could feel the heat of her skin. He felt a possessive growl rising in his throat and swallowed it back, fisting his hands by his side to keep from reaching for her.

What the hell? He had more control that this. A lot more. He had to or people got killed. Resisting a woman, even one that smelled like heaven, had never been a problem before. With Cary, it took an effort to resist pulling her close and burying his face in her neck to soak up her essence.

If he didn't know better, he'd think she was a witch, casting a lust spell on him.

His nostrils flared. That scent of hers…

It reached down inside him, calling to a deep instinct. As he breathed her in, his leopard whispered, *Mine.*

Out in the living room, wind-lashed hail whipped toward the bedroom without actually coming through the doorway. And behind that, a lightning bolt sizzled the floor.

"Sheldon didn't make this easy," he said, quirking a brow when she jumped at the sound of his voice.

"Are you dressed?" she asked without turning around.

He couldn't help smiling at the slight panic in her voice. "Yes."

"Okay. Stick close. Stay behind me and don't try to dodge around me. Got it? That's how we'll get out of here alive."

He frowned down at the top of her head. She must have some pretty powerful shields to get through that mess. But she wasn't a witch?

He grunted a noncommittal response, and she swung around to face him. The flash of heat in her eyes made his pulse kick.

"Listen, buddy," she said, her chin tucked back as she glared at him, "if you don't let me protect you, we're both dead. Okay? Don't go trying to be a hero. Just stay close and let me do what I came here to do."

She mumbled something unflattering under her breath as she turned back to the living room, and he had to fight a completely irrational urge to kiss her.

Over the course of the long day, with no sign of help from Jaxer, he'd had to face the possibility of his own death. His reaction to Cary might be a result of that, a need to reaffirm he was alive.

But as he breathed in the heady scent of her again, he wondered…

~

**Don't Miss
The Trouble with Black Cats and Demons
Cary Redmond, Book One**

The Cary Redmond Series
Out Now!

**Cary Redmond
Short Story
Collections**

BOOKS BY KAT SIMONS

THE CARY REDMOND SERIES

1 – The Trouble Black Cats and Demons

2 – The Trouble with Ghouls and Serial Killers

3 – The Trouble with Leopard Queens and Shifter Wars

4 – The Trouble with Baby Gods and Vampires

5 – The Trouble with Magic and Faery Curses

6 – The Trouble with Wizards and Old Enemies

COMING SOON

CARY REDMOND SHORT STORIES

When Cary Met Jaxer

When Cary Met Pickles

When Cary Met Angie

When Cary Met Lucy

When Cary Met Marianne

Cary and Deacon (Try to) Go On A Date

Date Night Take Two

Third Date's the Charm

Cary vs the Goblin King

Dinner with the Jones

Cary and the Cursed Jack-o-Lantern

Cary and the Demon Witch

Cary Goes to Hawaii

When Cary Met the Good Guys (Collection 1)

Dates, Dinners, and Other Disasters (Collection 2)

DEMON WITCH SERIES

Moonlit Strange (short story)

1 – Bone Lantern Witch

Romancing the Leopard: A Tiger Shifters-Cary Redmond Crossover Novel

TIGER SHIFTERS SERIES

1 – Once Upon a Tiger

2 – Along Came a Tiger

3 – Here There Be Tigers

4 – Her Tiger To Take

5 – To Tempt a Tiger

6 – Down Will Come Tiger

7 – To Catch a Tiger

8 – What a Tiger Wants

9 – Taming Her Tiger

Tiger Shifters Series Vol 1 (Books 1 - 3)

Tiger Shifters Series Vol 2 (Books 4 - 6)

JOAN OF KERRY SERIES

1 – Joan of Kerry: Joan and the Abhartach

ABOUT THE AUTHOR

Kat Simons earned her Ph.D. in animal behavior, working with animals as diverse as dolphins and deer. She brought her experience and knowledge of biology to her paranormal romance and urban fantasy fiction, where she delights in taking nature and turning it on its ear. Her Tiger Shifters series combines romance and the otherworldly with heart-pounding action adventure. Her latest urban fantasy romance series follows the adventures of Protector Cary Redmond as she tries to manage her personal life while saving the world. A lot.

For something a little different, Kat also publishes fantasy romance, science fiction romance, and the occasional hockey romance under the name Isabo Kelly.

After traveling the world, Kat now lives in New York City with her family. She is a stay-at-home mom and a full time writer.

For more on Kat and her future books:

Website: https://www.katsimons.com
Newsletter: http://eepurl.com/dxDRuH